WELCOME BACK TO YAWNEE VALLEY, its

green hills and cows, cows, cows. The grass grows, the hills roll, the cows moo. Who cares?

Well, these two.

This is Miles Murphy and Niles Sparks, the only members of a two-person secret club known to themselves and only themselves as the Terrible Two. (Miles is the one in a gas mask.)

The Terrible Two was a particular kind of secret club. The Terrible Two was a pranking club. And on this day, a Sunday, Miles and Niles were about to pull their latest prank.

On the day before this day, a Saturday, Miles and Niles had drawn up a list of things they'd need:

"Why would we need gas masks?" asked Niles. Miles and Niles were in their prank lab, a walk-in closet off Niles's bedroom whose four walls and ceiling had been covered in chalkboard paint so the Terrible Two could plot out their pranks.

Notice the maps. Notice the diagrams. Notice the crate full of black socks stuck in the corner.

The socks aren't important. But behind the socks was something very important. Behind the socks were fifty-eight words Miles and Niles lived by.

THE PRANKSTER'S OATH

- On my honor I will do my best
- To be good at being bad;
- To disrupt, but not destroy;
- To embarrass the dour and amuse the merry;
- To devote my mind to japes, capers, shenanigans, and monkey business;
- To prove the world looks better turned upside down;
- For I am a prankster.
- SO BE IT.

(If you're reading this book somewhere quiet, someplace alone where no one will hear you, feel free to raise your left hand—the prankster's hand—and say those words yourself.)

"And that's why we need gas masks," said Miles, who'd been talking this whole time.

"I don't think gas masks work like you think they work," said Niles.

"I think they work exactly like I think they work," said Miles.

"Well, yeah," said Niles. "That's the definition of thinking."

"*I'm* bringing a gas mask," said Miles. "And I'll bring one for you too. I'll bet you want it tomorrow."

Which is how we got here.

"Are you sure you don't want one?" Miles asked.

"Yes."

Niles pulled a clothespin out of his pocket and used it to clip his nostrils shut. He winced a little, because it hurt.

"The gas mask would be way more comfortable," said Miles.

"OK," said Niles.

"Plus it looks really cool."

Niles took a good look at Miles.

"Maybe," he said.

Miles and Niles laid the skateboards on the pavement. (Both skateboards belonged to Miles. This morning he'd ridden one over to the parking lot behind Danny's Diner. Niles had carried the other one. He didn't have very good balance.)

They put on their rubber gloves.

They pulled out their paintbrushes.

Then Miles reached into his backpack and removed the most important thing they needed for this morning's prank, something too important to include on their list, lest the list fall into the wrong hands, prompting questions, investigations, unmaskings, expulsions. It was the linchpin of the entire operation: a hunk of cheese wrapped tightly in plastic.

Yawnee Valley cows ate Yawnee Valley grass from Yawnee Valley hills to make Yawnee Valley milk. Some Yawnee Valley milk became Yawnee Valley cheese, for sale to customers

of the Yawnee Valley Creamery, purveyor of twenty-seven
varieties including:

American
Baby Swiss
Blue
Brick
Cheddar (mild)
Cheddar (medium)
Cheddar (sharp)
Cheddar (extra-sharp)
Chèvre
Colby
Colby-Jack
Cream Cheese
Farmer Cheese
Fresh Jack
Lacy Swiss
Monterey Jack
Mozzarella
Muenster
Parmesan

Pepper Jack
Pinconning
Provolone
Quark
Swiss
Teleme
White Cheddar

If you counted, you know that's only twenty-six kinds of cheese. But you might be interested to know that Yawnee Valley is also one of only four places outside Germany to make Limburger cheese, which Miles Murphy had purchased this morning, and which is famous for smelling like feet.

"Aw man," said Miles, unwrapping the cheese. "It smells like feet."

"That's the whole point," said Niles.

"Yeah, but I can smell the feet," Miles said, "through the gas mask."

Niles shrugged. "I tried to tell you. Gas masks block poison, not smells."

Miles lifted the gas mask off his face. "OK. You win. I'll take a clothespin."

Niles smiled. "I only brought one."

Leave it to Niles Sparks to prank his pranking partner in the middle of a prank.

"Good one," said Miles.

"Thanks," said Niles.

Miles looked a little queasy. He stared at the cheese. "It's even worse than I thought." He took a deep breath and held it.

Miles and Niles nodded to each other.

Then they got down on the skateboards, flat on their backs, and rolled under a yellow hatchback that belonged to their principal, whose name was Principal Barkin, and who ate lunch at Danny's Diner at the same time every Sunday.

A good prank required a good goat, and a good goat was someone who deserved to be pranked. Good goats were despots and tyrants, preeners and egomaniacs. Principal Barkin was a great goat, having:

1) insisted, in speeches and on signs he pasted around the school, that his power as principal be respected by students;

2) thrown tantrums whenever that power was called into question, his face turning

purple any time he got angry (which was often);

3) canceled this year's theme days, citing "frivolity," including Wacky Hair Day, Mustache Day, and Backward Day, leaving only Pajama Day (a compromise brokered by the class president, and even then Barkin had driven a tough bargain: On Pajama Day, school would start fifteen minutes early, "since students would have no need to get dressed");

4) committed several other heinous acts, including all the stuff from the first book.

It took ninety-three seconds to coat the car's undercarriage with Limburger cheese, and so in less than two minutes they were standing next to the car again.

"How does it smell?" Niles asked.

"Terrible," Miles said.

They grinned. Miles held up two fingers. Niles did too. They touched their fingertips together. It was the secret handshake of the Terrible Two, perfect for celebrating a prank well done.

"Let's go," said Miles.

But Niles wasn't finished.

"Hold on."

He checked to be sure nobody was looking, then smeared a layer of cheese on the vents right below the car's windshield.

It was the masterstroke.

Chapter
2

MEANWHILE, in Danny's Diner, two Barkins, Principal and Josh, were wrapping up Father-Son Brunch Time, part of Father-Son Sunday. Principal Barkin had implemented Father-Son Sunday to address ongoing concerns about Josh's behavior. The principal believed his son to be a prankster, and to correct this deviance, he'd settled on a carrot-and-stick approach. The "carrot" in this case was Father-Son Sunday, twelve hours set aside for father-son hikes, father-son games, and father-son brunches. Josh hated Father-Son Sunday. (He also hated carrots.) The "stick" in Principal Barkin's plan had been sending Josh to a military-themed summer camp, which would hopefully terrify him into obedience. Josh had loved it. (He also loved sticks—he'd spent all summer throwing them at people's heads.)

Principal Barkin unzipped his Principal Pack and pulled out a set of father-son flash cards on which he'd written questions designed to spark lively conversation between parents and adolescents.

"What is one goal you'd like to accomplish in your life-time?" Principal Barkin asked.

"I want to be a school principal," said Josh.

They were off to a great start!

"Mount Rushmore honors four presidents: George Washington, Thomas Jefferson, Abraham Lincoln, and Theodore Roosevelt. If you could add a fifth face to the monument, whose would you choose?"

"Mine."

What robust self-esteem!

"If you could teleport to anywhere in the world, where would it be?"

"Right now?"

"Yes, right now."

"That empty booth over there."

"Josh."

Josh stared out the window at a tree and thought about punching it.

"If you're not going to take this seriously," said Principal Barkin, "we can leave."

"Great," said Josh.

What had gone wrong, Principal Barkin wondered, gazing forlornly at his son, who was gazing malevolently at his father. Where had things gone awry between them? Was there a moment their relationship had spun off course? No! Of course not. You could not reduce something as complicated as the strain between a parent and child to a single moment, a particular event. Yet things had certainly taken a turn for the worse last spring, after Principal Barkin had both grounded and suspended Josh for various lies and misdeeds, forcing the boy to forfeit his position as class president. Then again, maybe it was just hormones!

"Hormones," Principal Barkin said aloud, befuddling his son. "Yes."

Josh had always been such a *sweet* boy by nature. Principal Barkin often thought fondly of those long-ago days when he would read little Josh a bedtime story, and Josh would call all the characters in the book nimbuses. Somewhere that sweetness must still flow through his veins, along with all those hormones.

But those days were long gone. The two Barkins rose and approached the cashier. Principal Barkin counted out exact change.

"Nice fanny pack," said the cashier.

Principal Barkin straightened, and his face turned the color of boysenberry jam. "What is your name?" he asked.

"Donna," said the woman, pointing to her name tag, which said DONNA.

"Well," said Principal Barkin, "*Donna*, I will have you know that this is not a 'fanny pack.' It's a Principal Pack."

"A principal pack?" Donna asked, then regretted asking.

"Yes. A Principal Pack. That's capital *P*, capital *P*—when you just said it now it sounded like lowercase. A Principal Pack is a pack, like this one, worn by a school principal, like me, containing everything necessary to successfully wield power in a school."

"Well, we're in a diner," said Donna.

"Donna," said Principal Barkin, "a principal does not stop being a principal when he leaves his school. A principal is a principal always. Even in a diner. Even on a Sunday."

"OK," said Donna, who did not really understand how she had gotten into this conversation, or why it was still happening. "Well, then nice Principal Pack."

"Thank you," said Principal Barkin.

Victory. He was glad Josh had seen that. It was the kind of role-modeling that Father-Son Sunday was all about.

Exercising authority put Principal Barkin in high spirits as he crossed the parking lot with his son. When Barkin was in high spirits, he sang, and today he sang his "Sunday Song," which was a new song he'd just made up about Sundays.

> "I'm very glad it's Sunday
> Because tomorrow it is Monday
> And Monday is the best day
> To start another school day."

He was on the second verse, which was the same as the first verse, when they got into his car and Barkin noticed the smell of feet.

This particular area of the parking lot smells a bit like feet, Barkin thought before firing up his hatchback and setting to work on his new song's bridge.

"Sunday, Sunday, Sunday, Sunday, Sunday, Sunday," he sang.

But the smell was still there when he pulled out of the

parking lot, and when he reached the stoplight at the intersection of Main and 3rd, Principal Barkin had to acknowledge the possibility that the smell was coming from the car.

"Something stinks," said Josh.

They rolled down their windows.

Hormones. Principal Barkin glanced at his son. Hormones! They caused moods. They caused rifts between fathers and sons. And they caused smells. Principal Barkin grew certain that hormones were the cause of all today's woes, including this particular woe, the foot smell, which was growing worse as the drive went on. In fact, it seemed that the stench was even stronger now that they had opened the windows, a fact Principal Barkin blamed on cross-ventilation. Cross-ventilation and hormones: the twin villains of this Father-Son Sunday.

Here was a delicate situation. As a school principal, Principal Barkin was an expert on adolescents, and he knew he needed to broach the issue of hygiene with sensitivity, lest he make his son ashamed of his body.

"Josh," said Principal Barkin, "I would like to say a few words about the importance of baths. Namely, do you take baths?"

"What? Yes!"

"Of course," said Principal Barkin. "Of course you do. And when you do, do you use soap?"

"Stop! Yes!"

"Wonderful," said Principal Barkin. "Terrific. And do you use soap on your feet?"

"You're blaming my feet?"

"Well," said Principal Barkin, "I am blaming feet. Somebody's feet. Your feet. Maybe blame is a strong word. But yes."

"What about *your* feet?"

"Josh," said Principal Barkin, "I have been with my feet for many years. I know my feet. And my feet have never smelled like this. Nevertheless! This is nothing to be ashamed of. As you grow from a boy to a man, your feet, naturally, are changing, growing larger, gaining hair, and yes, making new smells."

"Dad!"

"OK, OK, we don't need to talk about it. We will just drive home, and as soon as we get there, you will take a long bath and wash your feet. Please. Thank you."

Principal Barkin turned up the radio. As a courtesy to his son, he would pretend that the smell in the car was not unbearable, though it was. Principal Barkin attempted to arrange his face into a pleasant smile, and when that failed, into an expression of only mild disgust.

"Sunday, Sunday, Sunday, Sunday," he sang to the tune of the song on the radio.

Casually, Principal Barkin reached for the button to open the car's vents and hopefully blast out the smell once and for all.

Alas, the car filled with air tainted with the cheese Niles had smeared below the windshield.

Principal Barkin gagged. Wheels squealed as he pulled the car over in front of a pet store.

"All right! Out of the car. Foot check!"

"What?"

"Sit! Off with your shoes and socks!"

Muttering, Josh sat on the sidewalk and took off his shoes and socks.

Principal Barkin removed a bar of soap and a tiny water bottle from his Principal Pack.

"This is so weird," Josh said.

"I'm doing you a favor here, Josh. You will thank me for this one day!"

Principal Barkin took his son's right foot in his hand and bent down, soap in hand.

As he got close to the foot, he noticed something strange: It did not smell.

He got closer and sniffed deeply.

"Interesting," said Principal Barkin. "Very interesting."

Down the block, Miles and Niles stood, skateboards under their arms, jaws ajar.

"Well this one turned out great," said Miles. "Strange, but great."

Niles nodded. "Most definitely."

Chapter 3

THAT FATEFUL AUTUMN found nearly every day

punctuated by some prank perpetrated by the Terrible Two. September 30: The Big Chirp. October 15: The Cafeteria Calamity. But let's look closely at that parade of practical joking that was November 10, better known at Yawnee Valley Science and Letters Academy as school picture day.

School picture day is strange. You probably have your photo taken all the time, with cameras and phones, by family and friends. Still, once a year, you will be asked to carefully choose an outfit ("solid colors, in medium to dark shades for that *timeless* look"), put too much product in your hair ("schedule a haircut two weeks before your portrait"), and pick one of four backgrounds: Harvest Sunset (brown), Pacific Breeze (blue), Candy Apple (red), and Forest Trail (green). All four backgrounds will have a hazy white spiral running through them, so your picture will look like it was taken inside a wizard's cauldron. You will have the option of paying extra for a fifth background, Executive Gray (just regular gray), and you will wonder what kind of person spends ten bucks to get gray.

You will line up in the gym, clutching your order form—eight wallet size, four desk size, two 8 × 10s. You will file to the front of the line, where a huge camera flashes every few seconds. A bored man with a big beard will tell you a bad joke and snap a photo that will be given to grandparents and go up on your fridge. If your family loves it, they might put the photo on mugs or mouse pads or—worst of all—cell phone cases, so you will have to look at your school picture when your mom uses her phone to take pictures of you.

The best pictures capture who we truly are. School pictures capture who we are at school, on school picture day. Now sit down and smile. And don't blink! You don't want your school picture to turn out like this:

"Aw MAN!" said Stuart. (The kid in the picture is Stuart.) "I think I BLINKED!"

Mr. Yeager scratched his beard and looked at the camera. "Yes," he said. "You blinked."

"That ALWAYS happens to me," said Stuart. "I get FREAKED OUT about the FLASH!"

"Let's try this again," said Mr. Yeager. "Say 'Muenster.'"

"Aw MAN!" said Stuart. "Now I think I had my EYES CLOSED the WHOLE TIME."

"We'll try one more. Say 'Muenster.'"

"Looks good," said Mr. Yeager.

"COOL!" said Stuart.

"Next."

"Next."

"Next."

"Next."

"Can I have your order form?" asked Mr. Yeager.

"I don't have an order form," said Holly Rash.

"Did you forget it at home?"

"No. I don't really like having my picture taken."

"Then why did you wait in line?"

"I have to get one," said Holly. "I'm the class president."

"Next."

"Next."

"Muenster!" said Niles. "Instead of just 'cheese!' That's very good, Mr. Yeager. I remember when you made that joke last year, and I think it might have been even funnier this time around. You know, I always say that's the mark of a good joke: It gets a laugh no matter how many times you hear it."

"Uh-huh," said Mr. Yeager.

You may notice that Niles Sparks looks very different from when we last saw him. Notice the tie. Notice the well-combed hair. Notice the sash adorning his torso that says SCHOOL HELPER. That's because who Niles was at school—school picture day or not—was a very different person from who he truly was.

You already know that Niles Sparks was a prankster. He loved reading about pranks, thinking about pranks, and dreaming about pranks. But what you don't know (unless you've read *The Terrible Two*, in which case, hello again and feel free to skip the rest of this sentence) is that Niles Sparks avoided suspicion by pretending to be someone else.

"You'll notice I put all my activities on my order form, Mr. Yeager." Niles indicated a neatly written list in the lower right corner of the sheet. "School Helper, of course, but also captain of the safety patrol, lieutenant of the safety patrol, well, technically all the officers of the safety patrol, really the only member of the safety patrol besides Miles, who's just a cadet, although I'm urging him to show more initiative! I'm also president of the student behavior committee, chair of LADs, which is an organization I invented to ensure—"

"This is really more of a thing for whoever runs your yearbook," said Mr. Yeager. He popped a piece of gum in his mouth and gave Niles a tired look.

Niles knew the tired look Mr. Yeager was giving him right now. It was the look that said, "There's one of these kids at every school." What Niles understood was that people love to put things—songs and books and other people—into categories. There are so many books, and so many songs, and so many people in the world, and most of them are peculiar in one way or another. But it's a lot of work thinking about peculiar things, and so most people just sort the world into categories—"loud songs" or "funny books"—and then they don't have to think about these things anymore. Niles Sparks didn't want people thinking about him—he believed the best pranksters were invisible. And so every school day, Niles played the kiss-up, the toady, the persnickety twerp.

"Is that nicotine gum, Mr. Yeager?" asked Niles. "Congratulations on quitting smoking! I hope I wasn't too hard on you last year, but I also hope that I had something to do with your decision to get healthy! You might be interested to know that you were part of what inspired me to start Yawnee Valley Science and Letters Academy's first Student Anti-Smoking Society, which I've listed on my order form in the lower right-hand—"

"Next!"

"Get your hands away from me, Josh," Miles said. "You're sick."

"No, I'm not!" Josh said, then coughed.

"Josh!" said Ms. Shandy. "No bunny ears."

Josh Barkin patted Miles Murphy's head and turned to their homeroom teacher.

"Sorry, Ms. Shandy, but I think there's been a misunderstanding. You know how my dad, your boss, hates when students have mussed-up hair in their school pictures. I was just trying to fix the new kid's hair."

"I've been here for a year, Josh." It was exactly what the new kid would say. And even though Miles Murphy had been in Yawnee Valley for a year, he was still the new kid. When students talked about the field trip four years ago, or the pageant in kindergarten, or the time Coach O. did that dance at that one assembly, Miles had no idea what they were talking about. Maybe Miles was less new than he was twelve months ago, but when you're the new kid at school you stay the new kid until one day a newer kid comes, or you graduate with the rest of your class. And that was fine. Miles wanted to be the new kid for as long as possible. He wore "new kid" as a disguise. It explained why he spent so much time hanging out with a kid like Niles Sparks, and it obscured the fact that he was half of a pranking duo.

"Shut up, nimbus," said Josh. It was exactly what Josh would say, because he was always saying it.

The camera clicked. The flash flashed.

"Next."

"How about you show us that pretty smile, dear?" said Mr. Yeager.

"Dear?" said Ms. Shandy.

"Here's my card," said Mr. Yeager. "In case you ever need a photographer."

"I won't," said Ms. Shandy. "Bye."

"OK," said Mr. Yeager, fiddling with the backdrop. "Would the students who ordered Executive Gray please line up."

Only Josh stepped forward.

Josh put on a khaki cap he'd taken to wearing ever since coming back from camp. He had several bars and service ribbons fastened to the front of his shirt, which Miles and Niles suspected he'd bought at a military surplus store rather than earning.

"My dad, who is the principal of this school, is willing to pay for a more dignified portrait," Josh said to nobody in particular. (He was the last student to get his picture taken, and most of the class was milling around by the trophy case, dribbling basketballs Coach B. had specifically asked them not to dribble.) "Really this is more of a historic document, when you think about it, since one day I'll be principal of this school, just like my father, and his father, and his father before him. And also the father before him too." Josh counted on his fingers. "Plus one more. Five fathers. Forefathers. Five forefathers. Get it?" Mr. Yeager got it, but he did not laugh. "My dad says Executive Gray is the background of Barkins, because in his day they didn't even have color choices, and before that, pictures were black-and-white, so everything was sort of—"

Josh started coughing again.

Mr. Yeager backed away a bit. "Are you sick?"

"No!" Josh said. "Barkins don't get sick!"

"OK," said Mr. Yeager. "Because you sound sick."

"Shows what you know. A Barkin has never taken a sick day in the history of Yawnee Valley. My father, his father, all my five forefathers . . ." Josh paused for a laugh that never came.

"They all graduated with perfect attendance records. And I will too. It's quite simple: When you have the immune system of a future principal—"

"All right, let's do this," said Mr. Yeager.

Miles and Niles weren't even in the room to see their first prank of the day go off. They were on the way to a supply closet to carry out a safety patrol equipment check. One of the advantages of being on the safety patrol was always getting to miss class for equipment checks, strategy meetings, and traffic duty. Another advantage was unfettered access to the safety patrol supply closet, which was mostly full of stop signs and hard hats but also contained several canisters of reflective paint, which is meant to be sprayed on patrol equipment. It goes on clear but catches the light of oncoming headlights to ensure that crossing guards are visible to drivers. It also glows eerily when illuminated by, say, a camera flash, and is particularly effective against dark backgrounds. And so earlier that day, while Mr. Yeager was taking a cigarette break after photographing the first-graders (alas, he was having trouble quitting), Miles and Niles had snuck into the gym (they were supposed to be planning a bake sale for LADs) and doctored one of the backgrounds (you probably know which one). Anyone bumptious enough to pay for Executive Gray would find, when their school pictures came back, that they'd been visited by an uninvited guest.

Verily, it was a golden age of pranking.

And like any golden age, nobody knew it was happening until it was over.

YAWNEE VALLEY SCIENCE and Letters Academy

had a school picture day tradition that went back five principals. Each year the whole student body, the faculty, and the staff would assemble on the lawn in front of the school. Principal Barkin (in Yawnee Valley, there had always been a Principal Barkin) would take his place at the front of the group. Then everyone would tilt their heads toward a photographer standing on the gymnasium roof, who would snap a picture that would hang in the halls forever.

Here is the picture from 1883:

(The cow was not a student, but it frequently grazed on the grounds.)

From 1937:

Look, it's Jimmy Barkin! Known to his students as "the smiling principal" and to his family as "the family shame."

And 1972:

That's Current Principal Barry Barkin, then a student, standing next to his father, Former Principal Bertrand Barkin, then a principal, right there in the front row!

After lunch the school bell rang three times, which was the signal for everyone to gather.

"OK, EVERYONE!" Principal Barkin was shouting into a megaphone. "CLUMP UP! LET'S CLUMP UP! I WANT EVERYBODY CLUMPED THIS INSTANT, SO WE CAN GET BACK TO CLASS AS SOON AS POSSIBLE. AND WHILE WE ARE CLUMPING, I WOULD LIKE TO REMIND TEACHERS TO PLEASE TALK A LITTLE BIT FASTER THIS AFTERNOON TO MAKE UP FOR THE INSTRUCTIONAL TIME WE ARE LOSING BY TAKING THIS PHOTOGRAPH."

Students wandered the lawn trying to find their friends. Only half the teachers had made their way outside, and most of those were talking in a smaller clump over by the parking lot.

"ONE CLUMP!" said Principal Barkin. "ONE CLUMP RIGHT HERE ON THE FRONT LAWN. WHY IS IT THAT PEOPLE ARE ALWAYS CLUMPING UNTIL YOU ASK THEM TO CLUMP, WHEN THEY . . . THEY . . ."

"Scatter?" offered Niles, who was standing to Principal Barkin's right.

"YES! SCATTER. NO! DO NOT SCATTER. THAT

WAS THE END TO MY PREVIOUS SENTENCE, AND NOT AN INSTRUCTION TO SCATTER, WHICH IS THE OPPOSITE OF WHAT YOU SHOULD BE DOING."

Eventually everyone made their way to the front lawn. Barkin cut through the crowd and took his place at the front.

"Look!" said Stuart. "FLOWERS!"

"Yes." Barkin smiled. He'd noticed them on his way to work: Last night, on the lawn, a blanket of field violets had bloomed. Field violets! The state flower! And on picture day! Barkin considered it a sign from the universe: This truly would be Yawnee Valley Science and Letters Academy's best year. In fact, they were growing right next to the marquee, which read PRINCIPAL BARKIN SEZ: LET'S MAKE THIS OUR BEST YEAR. Sure, the marquee read this every year, but this year the marquee *meant it*. The violets blanketing the front of the lawn were a confirmation of everything the marquee said! Well, maybe not everything. The marquee also read PRINCIPAL BARKIN SEZ: FRIDAY IS PAJAMA DAY. But Friday *was* Pajama Day! So, yes! Everything!

"CAREFUL NOT TO DISTURB THE FLOWERS!" Barkin shouted into the megaphone. He couldn't have students trampling on a sign from the universe. And luckily these flowers had grown right in front of where the students normally stood for the all-school photograph. The universe was giving him the most photogenic sign possible. Yes!

"ALL RIGHT, STUDENTS," said Barkin. "NO FUNNY FACES. MAKE SURE YOUR HAIR ISN'T MUSSED. THIS IS REALLY MORE OF A HISTORIC DOCUMENT, WHEN YOU THINK ABOUT IT, SO COMPORT YOURSELF WITH DIGNITY AND GRACE AS YOU TILT YOUR HEADS UP TOWARD MR. YEAGER, WHO IS STANDING ON TOP OF OUR GYM."

"Uh, Barry?" Mr. Yeager cupped his hands in front of his mouth and shouted down at Principal Barkin. "I think there's something you ought to see."

"WHAT IS IT?" Principal Barkin pointed his megaphone up at Mr. Yeager.

"Flowers."

"I CAN SEE THE FLOWERS," said Principal Barkin. "THEY ARE WILD FIELD VIOLETS, OUR STATE FLOWER, AND THEY ARE A SIGN THAT WE'RE GOING TO HAVE OUR BEST YEAR."

"OK, but they're arranged."

"WHAT DO YOU MEAN?"

"Into letters. They're spelling something out."

For a moment, a very brief moment, Principal Barkin thought the violets might have spelled out something like BOVINE PRIDE! or YAWNEE VALLEY SCIENCE AND LETTERS ACADEMY: HOME OF ACADEMIC EXCELLENCE. He hoped, in that moment, Mother Nature herself was showing her school spirit.

But the moment died fast.

Principal Barkin realized he was in the middle of a prank.

His fingertips tingled. His face went purple.

"OH. WHAT DOES IT SAY?"

"You should just come up here and look yourself."

There was no way Barry Barkin was going to climb all the way on top of the gym to read some prankster's idea of a joke, while all the students and staff stared up at him, an embarrassed purple speck on a rooftop. There was no dignity in it. No power.

"JUST READ IT, DOUG."

Mr. Yeager scratched his beard. He shouted down: "The flowers say PRINCIPAL BARKIN SEZ: BUNION."

There were some nervous giggles.

"WHAT?"

"PRINCIPAL BARKIN SEZ: BUNION."

"I HEARD YOU THE FIRST TIME, DOUG."

"That's HILARIOUS," said Stuart. "What's a BUNION?"

"It's a big bony bump on a foot," said Principal Barkin, quietly, and not into the megaphone.

"Wait, what is it?" asked a kid named Scotty.

"A BIG BONY BUMP ON A FOOT!" Principal Barkin said into the megaphone.

"It SOUNDS like ONION!" said Stuart. "Like you have an ONION on YOUR FOOT!"

Everyone laughed. (It was maybe the first time people had laughed at one of Stuart's jokes.)

"I DO NOT HAVE AN ONION ON MY FOOT OR A BUNION ON MY FOOT!" said Principal Barkin. "THIS IS RIDICULOUS. I WOULD NEVER SAY BUNION."

"You just DID!" said Stuart.

"Twice," said Holly.

"STOP LAUGHING," said Barkin. (There was more laughing.) "ENOUGH. GUS, DIG UP THE FLOWERS."

The school janitor hurried off to get a shovel.

Niles approached cautiously. "Um, Principal Barkin?"

"Yes, Niles?" Principal Barkin was glad to see Niles's serious face and somber eyes. Here was a student who didn't go in for bunion pranks or onion jokes.

"I'm afraid Gus won't be able to dig up these flowers."

"Of course he can, Niles. Gus is a strong man and an excellent digger. Just last week he—"

"I don't doubt that," Niles said. "But these are field violets."

"Yes."

"The state flower."

"Niles, I know our state flower. I am a principal. I am filled with pride and knowledge of our state."

"Well, then you know that it's illegal to dig up a field violet. They're protected."

Principal Barkin became a deeper shade of purple (the color of a field violet, actually).

"OF COURSE I KNEW THAT!" Principal Barkin said. "I JUST FORGOT! GUS, DO NOT DIG UP THESE FLOWERS."

Gus hurried off to replace the shovel.

Principal Barkin paced furiously. What to do, what to do? Find this prankster, of course, and punish the prankster severely. But what to do now? With a photographer on the roof and the whole school watching?

"Maybe it's not so bad," said Miles Murphy, who'd come up to join Niles. "Maybe people will think it's like Paul Bunyan."

This was exactly the kind of foolishness that made Principal Barkin wonder why a kid like Niles hung out with a kid like Miles, besides the fact that he'd paired them up as school buddies last year.

"PAUL BUNYAN? *PAUL* BUNYAN? THEY'RE NOT EVEN SPELLED THE SAME WAY!"

"We could have a few kids lie on the ground over the *I* and the *O*," Miles said. "Turn them into a *Y* and an *A*!"

"Yeah," said Niles. "We could even have some other kids spell out 'PAUL' over there."

"PRINCIPAL BARKIN SEZ: PAUL BUNYAN? WHAT DOES THAT EVEN MEAN, MILES MURPHY?"

Miles shrugged. "I don't know. But what would you rather be saying in the all-school picture? Bunion? Or Paul Bunyan?"

Barkin stared at Miles. Then he picked up his megaphone. "ALL RIGHT, STUDENTS. LISTEN UP."

And so:

Chapter 5

LATER THAT AFTERNOON, Miles and Niles were
summoned to the principal's office.

Don't worry: They weren't in trouble. It was a Monday,
which meant it was time for a School Helper Check-In, a
weekly meeting Niles had invented as part of the duties of a
position Niles had also invented.

"Does he have to be here?" Principal Barkin nodded toward Miles, who stood next to a wastebasket with a pad and pencil in his hand.

"Miles is our School Helper Helper," said Niles, referring to another position he'd invented. "He takes minutes now, which frees up the minute-taking part of my brain for additional responsibilities."

"I suppose," said Principal Barkin.

"Principal Barkin," said Miles, "a little more than a year ago, you asked Niles to teach me everything he knew about being a great student. And I think we'd both agree that what Niles has

to teach could fill up a lifetime. I honestly believe I've grown, as a student and human, since you wisely assigned him to be my school buddy."

Principal Barkin grunted. The kid had a point. It had been a wise decision, one of his many wise decisions, and it was clear that the Miles Murphy standing in his office was a great deal better than the Miles Murphy who'd first walked through these doors last fall. His posture was straighter. His speech was more respectful. Sure, his hair might be a little mussed for Principal Barkin's liking. And those T-shirts. Principal Barkin wasn't sure about those T-shirts.

"First order of business," said Niles. "The first-graders made a papier-mâché cow in art class, and Miss S. thinks we should put it in the school entrance."

"Of course," said Principal Barkin. "It's adorable. Shows bovine pride. Approved."

"Great. Item two. Some of the drinking fountains are barely shooting water out at all, which leads to students putting their mouths directly on the metal, and with flu season fast approaching—"

"I'm sorry," said Principal Barkin. "I need to talk about the violets."

Niles nodded. "Of course."

Barkin held up a yellow legal pad covered in scrawls. "I've

been trying to work out who could have done it. Now, I know what you're probably thinking: Josh. But I think that camp this summer has helped . . . exorcise whatever got into him last year."

Niles's nod was sympathetic without expressing agreement.

"Now, this next one might be a little bit awkward," said Principal Barkin. He whispered: "What about Miles?"

"What!" said Miles.

"I was hoping you wouldn't hear that," said Principal Barkin. "This is just one reason I would have preferred that he not be at this meeting."

"It wasn't me," said Miles.

Barkin sighed. "The Miles Murphy motto. But no, I don't think it was, either. Last year's Miles, definitely. But current Miles, the Miles standing in front of me—you—I don't think so. A principal must trust his instincts, and my instincts are excellent. Which brings me to Stuart."

"Hmm," said Niles.

"Yes," said Principal Barkin. "Precisely what I was thinking. I'll write that next to his name here. 'Stuart: Hmm.' What about Holly?"

"Oh, no, I don't think so," Niles said quickly.

"She doesn't seem to have much respect for authority."

"She's the president of our class!"

"The perfect cover . . . I'm going to write 'Hmm' next to her name too. Maybe with an extra *m*."

"I wouldn't use an extra *m*."

"I already did. What about Scotty?"

"I don't know much about Scotty," said Niles.

"Neither do I," said Principal Barkin. "And yet he always seems to be around. Very strange. Very strange indeed. Six *m*'s."

"Hmm. Hmmm. Hmmmmmm," said Principal Barkin. He crumpled up the piece of paper, tossed it at the wastebasket, and missed, hitting Miles. "THIS IS NO GOOD!" he bellowed, looking up at his ceiling fan. "THIS IS NO GOOD AT ALL. WE ARE IN THE MIDDLE OF A PRANKING EPIDEMIC. I CANNOT HAVE THESE CHALLENGES TO MY POWER! THIS SCHOOL RUNS ON POWER. NOT ELECTRICAL POWER. I MEAN, OBVIOUSLY THE SCHOOL RUNS ON ELECTRICAL POWER, LITERALLY. BUT METAPHORICALLY THE SCHOOL RUNS ON MY POWER. PRINCIPAL POWER. MY POWER POWERS THIS SCHOOL METAPHORICALLY, JUST AS ELECTRICITY LITERALLY POWERS THAT FAN."

The fan squeaked but did spin.

"WHICH REMINDS ME, COULD WE GET GUS TO COME IN AND LOOK AT THIS FAN? I'M NOT SURE IT SHOULD BE SQUEAKING LIKE THAT."

Miles wrote it down:

Have Gus check on fan.

"I'm sorry you had to see that outburst, boys," said Principal Barkin. "But it's a peek at what it's really like to have immense power. It's not all pumpkin spice and candy corn." (Principal Barkin sometimes liked to keep his metaphors seasonal.) "Maybe one day you two will understand, when you're powerful principals like I am, although you won't be principals exactly like I am, since my son Josh will be principal of this school, and, Miles, if I'm being honest, you probably don't have what it takes to be a principal. Anyway, great power. It means you answer to nobody, only yourself, and it can be hard to look directly at yourself, especially when your self is so powerful, like staring into the—"

The phone on Principal Barkin's desk buzzed, and the school secretary's voice came from the speaker. "Phone call for you, Principal Barkin. It's your father."

Despite being interrupted, Barkin did not grow purple. Instead he went pale.

"Put him through," he said, and then picked up the receiver.

"BARRY, THIS IS YOUR FATHER, FORMER PRINCIPAL BARKIN." Miles and Niles could hear his voice from where they stood. "AM I INTERRUPTING SOMETHING?"

"Actually, yes," said Principal Barkin. "I'm in a meeting with—"

"WELL, WHY ARE YOU LETTING ME INTERRUPT YOU? A PRINCIPAL SHOULD NEVER BE INTERRUPTED. THAT'S ONE OF THE SEVEN PRINCIPLES OF PRINCIPAL POWER. THE THIRD PRINCIPLE, IN FACT, WHICH MEANS IT'S ONE OF THE THREE MOST IMPORTANT ONES. IF—"

"Father, you—"

"DO NOT INTERRUPT ME," said Former Principal Barkin. "I WILL NOT BE INTERRUPTED. DID YOU SEE THAT? EVEN AS A FORMER PRINCIPAL, I'M MORE OF A PRINCIPAL THAN YOU ARE. AND SPEAKING OF NOT BEING MUCH OF A PRINCIPAL, WHAT IS THIS I HEAR ABOUT A PRANK DURING TODAY'S ALL-SCHOOL PHOTOGRAPH?"

"How did you hear about that?"

"THAT IS NOT THE QUESTION," said Former Principal Barkin. "AND THE ANSWER TO THAT NON-QUESTION IS THAT A GOOD FORMER PRINCIPAL MAINTAINS HIS SECRET SOURCES."

"Was it Mr. Yeager?"

"YES. BUT THAT IS NOT THE POINT. NOW, HERE IS WHAT *IS* THE QUESTION. THE QUESTION IS, HOW COULD YOU LET THIS HAPPEN?"

"Well—"

"THE ALL-SCHOOL PHOTOGRAPH IS A HISTORIC DOCUMENT."

"I know, but—"

"AND THIS YEAR THE ALL-SCHOOL PHOTOGRAPH WILL RECORD A SPECTACULAR PRANK, WHICH IS AN AFFRONT TO POWER, AND TO THE BARKIN NAME, WHICH IS SYNONYMOUS WITH POWER."

"Yes, but—"

"AND DO YOU KNOW WHAT THE SAD THING IS, BARRY? THE SAD THING IS THAT MAYBE THIS YEAR'S PHOTOGRAPH, WHICH RECORDS AN AFFRONT TO POWER, IS HISTORICALLY ACCURATE.

BECAUSE I HEAR FROM MY SECRET SOURCES THAT THERE HAVE BEEN A LOT OF PRANKS LATELY. AN EPIDEMIC."

"I don't know if I'd use the term 'epidemic.'"

"OH, LET'S SEE. A TEACHER'S DESK FASTENED TO THE CEILING? A CLASS TURTLE PAINTED BLUE? AND THEN OF COURSE THE BUSINESS LAST YEAR WITH THE COWS, WHICH IS TOO EMBARRASSING TO MENTION."

"You actually interrupted my investigation—"

"I DIDN'T CALL TO HEAR EXCUSES. I CALLED TO LET YOU KNOW THAT, ACCORDING TO OTHER SECRET SOURCES, AND I HOPE IT IS CLEAR THAT I MAINTAIN MANY SECRET SOURCES, YOUR LEADERSHIP, OR LACK THEREOF, WILL BE THE MAIN TOPIC OF THE SCHOOL BOARD MEETING THIS WEDNESDAY."

"What?"

"THAT IS ALL. GIVE JOSH AND SHARON MY LOVE."

For a few seconds Principal Barkin was too stunned to hang up the phone. When his eyes refocused, he saw Niles and then Miles, who were too stunned to not look stunned.

"I probably should have asked you to leave while I took that call," said Principal Barkin. "Let's continue this meeting next week."

Miles and Niles quietly left the office. They walked through the teachers' lounge and into the hall. It was a few minutes before either of them spoke. But eventually Miles asked a question. It was a question he never thought he would ask.

"Niles," he said, "should we feel bad for Principal Barkin?"

NO," Niles said.

It was the same answer he'd given in the hallway, and then after school in the prank lab. Now he was giving it again, while he and Miles walked along Jefferson Street in downtown Yawnee Valley. They passed a brick bank, a feed shop, a seed shop, and an ice cream parlor.

"No," Niles said yet again. "Because think about it." (Niles had been thinking about it.) "Pranks were invented to unstuff stuffed shirts. To pop overinflated balloons. To embarrass the dour. And what's Principal Barkin if not a dour balloon in a stuffed shirt?"

"Yeah," Miles said. "A purple balloon."

"Exactly! Look, we witnessed something weird in there today. But what if Robin Hood had accidentally seen the Sheriff of Nottingham crying during 'Greensleeves'? Does that mean the sheriff gets to overtax the poor? Should the Merry Men disband and go work for the Crown?"

Miles and Niles had paused in front of the ice cream parlor, and they stopped talking for a second so they could inhale the smell of waffle cones.

"Anyway," said Niles, "we can go to the school board meeting and testify on Principal Barkin's behalf. We'll make sure nothing happens to him. Everything will be fine. Now, let's get to this week's étude."

For the past few months, Miles and Niles had engaged in a series of exercises designed to develop their pranking muscles: the études—or as Miles liked to call them, the Hey Dudes. Lately they'd been exchanging a set of objects. They each had twenty-four hours to design a prank using only those materials. Last week Miles had given Niles a soccer ball, a bicycle pump, and a tube of industrial-strength superglue. Too easy. This week Niles had something really special.

"Here you go."

He held out a big spool of thread.

Miles stared at the thread. "Thread? That's all?"

That wasn't all. This wasn't just thread. Niles had found this spool in his mom's sewing kit, and he couldn't wait to tell Miles what it did. "This isn't just—"

"I've got an idea," Miles said.

"Wait," said Niles. "You don't know—"

But Miles was already approaching a man wearing denim shorts and a shirt that said THE EDGE: WORLD'S HARDEST TRIATHLON.

"Excuse me, sir." Miles smiled. "My friend and I are doing

a math project where we have to measure various streets in Yawnee Valley. Would you be able to help us?"

The man looked skeptical. He opened his mouth but Miles kept talking.

"It will only take a minute. All you have to do is stand here and hold this end of our thread." Miles put on a vulnerable expression. "It's really important for our grade."

He thrust the thread toward the man.

"Sure, I guess," the man said.

"Thank you! Thank you!" Miles said. Holding the spool in his hand, he backed away. "We won't be long, sir! Just stay there and don't move. We need an exact measurement!" He and Niles disappeared around the corner and took off down the street, the spool unwinding in Miles's hand. They slipped behind a coffee shop, turned down an alley, and nearly made it to a fire escape before the thread ran out.

"We need something to tie it to," said Miles, holding the thread taut. "The fire escape!"

"Wait!" said Niles. "Wait. I have a plan."

A man in a gray suit came around the corner, talking on his phone.

"Ha, ha!" Niles said. (He actually said, "Ha, ha!")

Niles waved and put on a cornball grin as the man approached. "Sorry to interrupt your call, sir!"

The man looked irritated. "Hold on," he said into his phone, which he kept near his ear.

"My friend and I are doing a math project where we have to measure various streets in Yawnee Valley," said Niles. "Would you be able to hold on to the end of this thread for a moment? You'd be able to continue your phone conversation and help two students with their math grade at the same time!"

The man seemed perplexed, but Niles was already handing over the thread.

"Please just hold it tight and stand right here," he said. "We won't be a moment."

As Miles and Niles walked out of the alley, Niles called out a series of numbers. "Fifty point three," he said, and Miles nodded seriously. "Sixty point eight five." They made it to the corner. "Thank you, sir!" Niles shouted. "We'll be right back!"

As soon as they were out of sight, they sprinted back to Niles's house.

"Incredible!" said Niles, in the safety of the prank lab.

"Amazing!" said Miles.

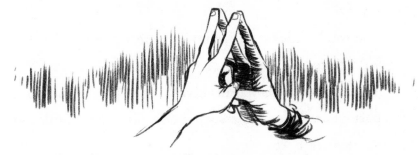

Their faces were flushed with the joy of a prank well done, their bellies full of tangerines. (The Terrible Two liked to celebrate with feasts.)

"But, Miles," said Niles, "I didn't even get to tell you what that thread does."

Miles shrugged. "It's thread, right?"

Niles smiled. "Nope. Hold on."

Niles left the prank lab and returned with another spool.

"Read the label," he said.

"My mom uses it for quilts and stuff," explained Niles. "It dissolves in water."

"Seriously?"

"Yep."

"Cool."

Niles frowned. "I just wonder if the prank needed to include dissolving."

"No way!" Miles said. "That was a great prank."

Niles paced. "It was. It was."

Miles sighed. This was his least favorite part of the études: the part where Niles endlessly pondered how the prank could have gone better.

Niles picked up the chalk and aimlessly drew on the wall. "I kind of feel like it's a Chekhov's gun thing, you know?"

"I *don't* know."

"Chekhov was this Russian—"

"And he had a gun?" Miles sat up straight. "Was he a spy?"

"No, he was a writer. And he thought that if you introduced a gun into a story, it has to go off before the end. He meant stories should contain nothing extraneous, nothing irrelevant. It feels like the same thing is true of pranking, right? If the thread can dissolve, it should dissolve, or else the dissolving is extraneous."

"I was just trying to keep it simple, man."

Niles snapped the chalk in half. "Occam's razor!"

Miles rolled his eyes. "Another Russian guy?"

"No. He's English. And he thought the simplest solution was the best. A more complicated solution might work, but if you have a choice, a simpler one is preferable. So what's more powerful? Chekhov's gun or Occam's razor?"

"Probably the gun," said Miles. "It's a gun."

Niles ignored him.

"Maybe Chekhov's gun is better for stories, and Occam's razor is better for pranks." Niles nodded. "Yes, I think that's right."

He pulled out a notebook and started writing something down.

"What is this music?" Miles asked.

"It's Bach!" Niles said. "On a Moog synthesizer!"

"I don't know why I even asked," said Miles.

Miles peeled a tangerine with his Swiss Army knife.

"You know you can just use your thumbnail," Niles said.

"I know," said Miles.

Outside, a horn honked three times. It was Miles's mom.

"I have to go," said Miles. "Me and my mom are going out to dinner."

✦ ✦ ✦

That night, Niles made himself spaghetti and meatballs. He ate in his room and put on the Bach again. Twirling noodles around his fork, Niles sat and thought about that afternoon's prank. How long had the two men stood there? Which one had first decided to follow the thread and see where it was going? Where did they meet? What had they said to each other? There was something beautiful about a prank that paid off when you weren't around. Sure, it was fun to see the chaos you created. But a prank like this afternoon's afforded the prankster a peculiar kind of pleasure. You could sit and picture the strange happenings you'd brought about in the world. There were so many ways it could have played out, and Niles sat in his big chair and imagined as many as he could. All those possibilities, and all of them strange and delightful. The mental exercise focused an unquiet mind (and that day Niles's mind was unquiet). Thinking about the thread kept Niles from thinking about things he'd rather not think about.

NOBODY LIKED TO GO TO MEETINGS of the

Yawnee Valley School Board, not even the Yawnee Valley School Board. That Wednesday, only two of its five members were in attendance: Mr. Karl Sykes and Mrs. Melinda Chunch. Mr. Sykes wore an unappealing mustache, and so did Mrs. Chunch. The audience was small too. Miles Murphy, Niles Sparks, and Barry Barkin sat in the basement of the library, surrounded by twenty-seven empty chairs. Miles had even worn a tie for the occasion.

Principal Barkin gave Miles and Niles two thumbs-up. "The dynamic duo! Here to save the day! Looks like we've got the naysayers outnumbered, boys, 3–0."

Mrs. Chunch banged a gavel loudly, which she loved doing, and which was really the only reason she'd shown up.

"This should be interesting," Niles said. (It was the first time anyone had ever said this about a Yawnee Valley School Board meeting.)

It took a while to get to the interesting part. First there was a roll call, which took much longer than it should have. The board approved the minutes of the last meeting and the agenda for the next meeting. Mrs. Chunch read aloud the mission statement of the Yawnee Valley Unified School District (Principal Barkin grunted approvingly throughout the recitation, and when Mrs. Chunch finished, he applauded a little bit). Then came votes on whether to approve the new Recess Restriction Policy (two ayes), the Supplemental Services Memorandum of Understanding (two ayes), and a contract to refinish the floors of the gym at Yawnee Valley Science and Letters Academy (two ayes). If you think this paragraph was boring to read, imagine what it was like to sit in a metal folding chair while it actually happened.

Thirty-six minutes into the meeting came AGENDA ITEM K: OPEN PUBLIC HEARING ON THE ADMINISTRATION OF BARRY BARKIN.

Mr. Sykes read from a crisp sheet of paper. "There has been recent concern over Principal Barkin's stewardship of Yawnee Valley Science and Letters Academy, arising first with the cancellation of school on April first of last year, and increasing due to an ongoing epidemic of practical jokes—"

"Epidemic," muttered Principal Barkin.

"—an epidemic apparently unchecked by principal power.

This meeting invites members of the community to speak about the Barkin administration."

"The floor is now open," said Mrs. Chunch, banging the gavel.

"You didn't need to bang the gavel for that, Melinda," said Mr. Sykes.

"Chairwoman Chunch," said Mrs. Chunch.

"Acting Chairwoman," said Mr. Sykes. "Only because Jeff isn't here."

"Which, according to bylaw 34(d), makes me chair. I can bang the gavel at my discretion."

"If you bang the gavel willy-nilly," said Mr. Sykes, "it loses all meaning."

Mrs. Chunch looked right at Mr. Sykes and banged her gavel some more.

"That's just great," said Mr. Sykes. "Why don't you show some restraint."

"You're just jealous of my gavel," said Mrs. Chunch.

Mr. Sykes didn't really have anything to say to that.

Mrs. Chunch cleared her throat and banged the gavel again. "The floor is now open. Citizens of Yawnee Valley are invited to approach the microphone."

Miles was the first to speak. He walked up to a microphone stand that stood a few feet in front of the table where the school board sat.

"I don't really think we need a microphone," he said, looking around the room.

"We always use microphones," said Mrs. Chunch, into her microphone. "Bylaw 17(t)."

"OK," said Miles. He took out a sheet of binder paper. "My name is Miles Murphy."

The speakers squeaked hideously.

"There's something wrong with his microphone," said Mr. Sykes. "Gus, could you bring us a new microphone?"

Gus, who worked at the county library most nights, hurried in with a new microphone and began fiddling with cords.

"I really think I can do this without it," Miles said.

Mrs. Chunch raised the gavel to silence him.

"Testing, testing," Gus said into the microphone. "Four score and seven years ago. A screaming comes across the sky. Such were the joys. When we all, girls and boys, in our youth-time were seen on the Ecchoing Green." He gave the table the OK. "This one should work, folks."

Mrs. Chunch banged the gavel. "Resume."

"My name is Miles Murphy," Miles said. "From my first day at school last year, Principal Barkin has been a welcoming presence and a wise and guiding authority figure. He learned my name right away and was a friendly face while I became accustomed to my new school. Principal Barkin believes in my potential and makes sure I achieve my best. And he introduced me to my best friend."

Only the first and last sentences of this speech were true, but that was fine.

Mrs. Chunch smiled. "Thank you, Miles."

"Thank you," Miles said. He took his seat.

Principal Barkin leaned over and whispered, "A little short, Miles, and light in terms of content related to my principal power, but altogether not too bad."

Niles Sparks was the next to step up. "Lady and gentleman of the school board, I'm here today to tell you about my hero. A great man. A powerful man. A principal. Principal Barkin."

"Here we go," Barkin said, pumping his fist a little.

Niles Sparks praised the leadership of Principal Barkin in a seven-minute presentation, enhanced by visual aids intended to supplement the school board's understanding: charts, photographs, and even a diorama.

When he was finished, the school board gently applauded. Barkin cried a little bit.

"Nice one," Miles said when Niles sat down.

"I think we did well," said Niles. They gave each other a high two.

"What's that?" Barkin asked. "A secret handshake? Neat! I think I missed it. Will you show it to me?"

"Anyone else?" asked Mrs. Chunch.

Barkin stood hastily. "Me!" he said. He buttoned his blazer and came up to the microphone.

"Let's do this, Barry," he said to himself.

Principal Barkin was proud of his many accomplishments as a principal, but he was probably proudest of his mastery of a rhetorical mode beloved by principals: the power speech. A power speech is meant to impress the listener and elevate the speaker. And last night Principal Barkin had stayed up late, cooking up a doozy. There was no doubt: This was the speech of his career. Words had flowed. Power had radiated. Metaphors had popped into his mind like . . . like . . . like a self-cranking Jack-in-the-box, but just the Jack, obviously, not the box, the Jack was the metaphor, and it wasn't a creepy Jack, the kind that was scary, with a creepy clown face, but a nice, smiling Jack, with a face that was beautiful and simple, like his metaphors.

"DISTINGUISHED SCHOOL BOARD MEMBERS, I AM PRINCIPAL BARKIN, THE PRINCIPAL IN QUESTION." The speakers squealed.

"There's no need to shout," said Mrs. Chunch. "You have a microphone." She was hard to hear. Barkin had blown out the sound system.

"Gus!" shouted Mr. Sykes.

The back doors opened, but instead of a smiling Gus, there stood a frowning Former Principal Barkin.

The room gasped audibly, which was impressive since there were only five gaspers.

Bertrand Barkin strode to the front of the room.

"Sit down, Barry," he said.

Barry Barkin backed up and took a seat in the front row.

Former Principal Barkin adjusted some knobs on an AV cart and tapped the microphone. The speakers were back on.

"Melinda, Karl, my apologies for showing up in the middle of things. I'm sure you'll understand that after I retired from the school board, I promised myself not to be present at any more of these meetings than I had to be."

Mrs. Chunch and Mr. Sykes chuckled.

"Let's be brief. I don't want to waste any more of your time. As you just witnessed, my son lacks discipline. And so his school lacks discipline. The pranks at Yawnee Valley Science and Letters Academy are out of control. They're cutting into instruction time. And they're making our district a laughingstock. I happen to know from colleagues that we're the butt of many a joke in the teachers' lounges over in Cherry Valley. No father likes to speak ill of his own son. But I feel I am a man with two children, and one of them is Yawnee Valley Science and Letters Academy."

"And Bob," Principal Barkin said from the front row.

Bertrand Barkin glared at Barry. "Yes. Bob. Three children. Barry and Bob and the school. And the school is in crisis. And in a crisis, we must take action. And so I submit the following proposal: that Principal Barkin take an involuntary, indefinite leave of absence."

"You want to fire me?" said Principal Barkin.

"That's your second interruption," said Former Principal Barkin. "And that's not what I said."

"It's pretty much what you said."

"It's not what he said," said Mr. Sykes, looking at his notes. "He said 'an involuntary, indefinite leave of absence.'"

"Now, just a minute, Bertrand," said Mrs. Chunch. "Who would replace him?"

"A powerful principal who can put an end to all this nonsense." Former Principal Barkin leaned into the microphone. "Me."

"WHAT?" said Principal Barkin.

"Order!" said Mrs. Chunch.

"Bang! Bang!" went the gavel.

"I hereby submit the following motion for a vote," said Former Principal Barkin.

"Can he even do that?" said Principal Barkin.

"Yes," said Mr. Sykes.

"That, effective immediately, Principal Barkin take an involuntary, indefinite leave of absence, and that I, Bertrand Barkin, take over in his stead."

"Aye," said Mr. Sykes.

"Nay," said Mrs. Chunch.

It was a tie.

According to bylaw 98(j), in the event of a tie, the deciding vote is cast by the school board's member-at-large.

The school board's member-at-large was Bertrand Barkin.

He voted in favor of his own proposal.

Barry Barkin was out of a job.

SO, THAT DIDN'T GO WELL," said Miles Murphy.

"No, it didn't," said Niles Sparks.

He and Niles were eating pizza in Niles's room.

"What's this music?" Miles asked.

"Zither!" said Niles.

"Right," said Miles. He swallowed his bite. "So what do we do now?"

Niles picked a piece of pepperoni off his slice and put it on the side of his plate for later.

"What do you mean?"

"What do we do about Principal Barkin?"

Niles smiled. "Well, we welcome him to Yawnee Valley Science and Letters Academy, of course. Did you see him in there? He's a skunk."

"A skunk?"

"A rotten rascal just asking to get pranked. Mean and humorless. The best kind of target. A good goat is rare, but a skunk? Pranksters wait their whole lives for someone like Bertrand Barkin to come around."

"Cool," said Miles. "But that wasn't the Principal Barkin I was asking about."

"I know."

The boys chewed.

The Barkin Miles was talking about, Barry Barkin, sat behind the wheel of his yellow hatchback, parked in the driveway of his house. The music was turned way down, and he was having a long talk with himself.

"This is a good thing, Barry," he said. "This is probably the best thing that has ever happened to you. You've been a principal for over fifteen years. Think of all you've missed! You haven't had any time for your projects! And I know what you're thinking, Barry. You're thinking, 'What projects?' But that's just it! You haven't even had the time to think of the projects you're interested in. That's Project #1: Start a list of projects."

He unzipped his Principal Pack, which after the board meeting was now technically just a fanny pack, and pulled out a notebook. The cover of the notebook said

PRINCIPAL IDEAS, the first word of which he crossed out and replaced.

He flipped past pages he'd already written on—WAYS TO MENTOR MYSELF, LEADERSHIP TECHNIQUES FOR LEADING TOMORROW'S LEADERS, PARENTS WHO HAVE NEVER VOLUNTEERED—and got to a blank page. PROJECT LIST, he put at the top.

He tapped his teeth with the tip of his pencil.

He wrote:

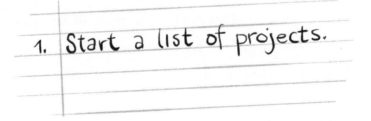

Then he put a big check mark next to it.

"Barry," he said, "the starter pistol has fired, and you're off to the races!"

He began writing furiously now.

✓1. Start a list of projects.

2. Discover who you truly are, through projects.

3. Figure out why this car still smells like feet.

◆ ◆ ◆

"It does feel like it's sort of our fault," said Miles.

"Look," said Niles, "the picture-day prank wasn't nasty or cruel. We had no intention of destroying anything! We couldn't know Barkin's dad was a skunk! And it was his dad who got him canned, not us. That whole mess at the school board meeting, that was between the two of them. There was nothing we could do. Miles, we have to move forward and do what we do best. School starts in less than fourteen hours. We should have something ready for Old Man Barkin first thing in the morning."

"Well. OK."

"OK," said Niles. "Now, what do you know about the Scoville scale?"

Distance is measured in feet. Weight is measured in pounds. Milk is measured in gallons, or imperial teaspoons. The height of a horse is measured in hands. The brightness of light is measured in lumens. And the spiciness of a hot pepper is measured in Scoville heat units.

Here is a bell pepper.

It scores a zero on the Scoville scale. It's not spicy at all.

Plenty of people have trouble with jalapeños, which rate up to 10,000 Scoville heat units.

Serranos are getting serious: 25,000 SHUs. Bird's-eye chilies clock in somewhere above 100,000 SHUs. You can find them in curries and they look like this:

The next time you get Thai food, dare somebody to eat one.

Moving up, we have the habañero (300,000 SHUs), the ghost pepper (1 million SHUs), and the Trinidad Moruga Scorpion (1.2 million SHUs).

And then there is the hottest pepper in the world. It fries tongues, burns throats, makes stomachs want to leap from bodies. If a pepper can be evil, this pepper is evil.

Its name is the Carolina Reaper.

A Carolina Reaper is red and bumpy. It has a bright green stem at its top and an impish tail curling off its bottom. Take a look at this beauty:

This pepper is from a plant that had been growing on Niles's windowsill for a year and a half.

"I've been saving these peppers for a special occasion," he said.

Niles wiped his hands off on a napkin and put on a pair of rubber dishwashing gloves. He plucked a fat little fruit from the bottom of the plant and gingerly set it down on top of the table between Miles and himself.

"Over 2.2 million Scoville heat units," he said. "That's 220 times hotter than the hottest jalapeño."

"Whoa mama," said Miles.

They stared at the pepper for a few seconds, silently, in awe.

"Should we try it?" Miles asked.

Niles grinned. "Really?"

"I mean, don't we kind of have to? Just to see?"

"Oh man," said Niles. "OK."

Miles pulled his Swiss Army knife from his pocket and split the pepper in two. Niles picked up his half with a gloved hand. Miles speared his with the knife and held it inches from his mouth.

"One," said Miles.

"Two," said Niles.

"Three," said Miles.

They each nibbled off a tiny bite.

Why oh why oh why did they do it? Immediately a numbness spread from the taste bud on the tip of Niles's tongue across his tongue's whole top. Then the bottom went numb, and the inside of his cheeks. If only the numbness had lasted: In less than a second his whole mouth was aflame. Niles had to get the pepper out of his mouth. He swallowed. Bad idea. It was like his esophagus got napalmed.

Meanwhile, Miles had begun hiccuping furiously.

"My insides are melting," he said between spasms.

"Your eyes are bugging out!" Niles said.

"Your whole face is red!" said Miles.

"You're crying!" said Niles.

"We're both crying!" said Miles.

Niles stripped off his rubber gloves and rubbed his eyes furiously. He was sweating. His head was hot and getting hotter. It was awful. It was spectacular.

"Oh man oh man."

"I need water!" Miles said.

"That makes it worse!" said Niles.

"I need something!" Miles said.

"Ice cream!" said Niles.

He ran from the room and returned in less than a minute with a tub full of mint chip and two spoons.

They tore off the lid and dug in. Ice cream ran out the sides of their mouths.

"My mouth feels better, but my whole body's burning up," Niles said.

"Mine too," said Miles. He ripped off his shirt.

"Good idea," said Niles.

Miles ran to the window and threw it open. He and Niles lay shirtless on the floor, rolling around with mouths full of ice cream, laughing and crying, saying, "Why oh why oh why."

BERTRAND BARKIN WAS THE KIND of man who wore a belt and suspenders. Usually, this is just a saying, but in Bertrand Barkin's case it was actually true. He wore a belt, and he wore suspenders. On the same day. At the same time. Of course, he was also the kind of person the saying refers to: a puritanical twit, an overstarched prig, a prude, a killjoy, a fuddy-duddy, a skunk.

This particular skunk was having a great morning. It felt good to put on the old belt and suspenders, drive to the school, and pull into the principal's parking space. It felt even better to be in the old office. He hung up his coat on the old rack and sat behind the old desk, in the old chair. Bertrand frowned. The old chair was at a new height. That needed to be fixed. The chair sighed as Bertrand lowered it three and a half inches. Perfect.

Bertrand nodded. The place still smelled the same. Wet wool and burnt coffee. There was a faint whiff of bergamot —Barry had always had a weakness for Earl Grey tea—but Bertrand could clear that up by brewing up a pot of the old Bertrand blend. He removed a zippered bag of coffee grounds from his briefcase and poured some into the machine. The switch glowed orange and the stuff started to drip.

Bertrand Barkin rinsed out a mug. WORLD'S GREATEST PRINCIPAL. Well, that was finally true again.

All right, it was time to make this official. He reached over the desk and removed the brass nameplate that said PRINCIPAL BARKIN, replacing it with a brass nameplate that said PRINCIPAL BARKIN.

"Barkin's back," he said to himself.

"Specifically, Bertrand Barkin," he said.

Bertrand allowed himself thirty seconds of leisure, during which he surveyed the portraits of Barkins that lined the walls: Thadius, Roger, himself, and Barry. All the Principal Barkins, except one, a lenient principal who'd brought shame upon the Barkin name and whose portrait Bertrand had ordered removed. That principal's name was Jimmy, although Bertrand had called him Father, although Jimmy had wanted to be called Dad.

Bertrand wondered: Should there be two portraits of himself on the wall, since he had now been principal twice? Or should he take down Barry's portrait, erasing that little blip, the blank spot in Bertrand's period of power?

Power. That reminded him. Bertrand pulled out a manual typewriter, which he'd lugged with him this morning.

Feeding a piece of yellowed paper into the platen (he'd brought the paper from home too), Bertrand felt the old spirit waxing within him. He had a hunch these kids had never heard a real power speech before. Well, he would soon remedy that. Things were going to change around here, and it was important to start things off on just the right note.

THE STUDENTS FILED into the auditorium. "What's happening?" Holly asked.

"Principal Barkin got FIRED," said Stuart.

"Technically he's taking an involuntary, indefinite leave of absence," said Niles.

"So he got fired," said Holly. "What for?"

"Well," said Miles. He nervously fiddled with the plastic bag in his pocket.

Josh shoved his way into the line and the conversation. "What are you nimbuses talking about?"

"Your dad," Holly said.

"That nimbus?" said Josh.

"He's your DAD," said Stuart.

"Whatever. Everyone says I take after my grandfather."

"Who's everyone?" Miles asked.

"My grandfather."

Bertrand Barkin perched on the stage, sipping his coffee, watching the kids pass below him.

Miles nodded at Niles.

It was time.

Niles broke from the line and climbed up onto the stage.

"Hello, Principal Barkin!" Niles smiled cheerfully and held out his hand. "Welcome to Yawnee Valley Science and Letters Academy! Or more accurately, welcome back!"

Bertrand Barkin switched the mug from his right hand to his left and gave Niles a joyless handshake. "And you are?"

"Niles Sparks!" said Niles Sparks. "I wanted to give you this apple," he said, removing a Red Delicious from his jacket pocket and thrusting it toward Barkin's left hand.

Barkin switched the coffee mug again and took the apple.

"On the first day of school, I like to give an apple to everyone on the faculty and staff, but you weren't here then! So, happy *your* first day of school."

Niles extended his hand again. Bertrand Barkin, both hands full, was briefly flustered, then set his coffee down on the edge of the stage so he could shake Niles's hand.

(This was precisely the moment Miles was passing by.)

"If you're anything like your son," Niles said, looking Barkin in the eye, "I know you'll be a terrific principal."

Barkin snorted. "I am nothing like my son."

Niles shrugged nervously. "Well, I'm sure you'll be a terrific principal nevertheless."

"Yes." Barkin bent over and retrieved his coffee. "Thank you. You are dismissed."

Niles, grinning uncomfortably, backed up and hopped off the stage. He hustled over to rejoin his class.

Miles was saving him a seat. "That looked intense," Miles said.

"It was like shaking hands with a lizard. How'd it go?"

"The eagle is in the nest," Miles said.

"The cow is in the barn," said Niles.

"The cat is in the litter box," said Miles.

What they meant was this: The hot pepper was in the coffee mug. Barkin's beverage was now off the charts, in terms of SHUs.

Bertrand Barkin approached the podium.

He set his mug down next to the microphone.

Miles and Niles settled into their chairs.

"Good morning, children," said Principal Barkin. "I am your new principal. My name is Principal Barkin. And let me begin by saying that Pajama Day is canceled."

A discontented murmur ran through the auditorium.

Holly looked around at the faces of her fellow students. She stood up.

"But, Principal Barkin," she said. "The last Principal Barkin—"

Barkin slammed his fist onto the podium. "SILENCE! I WILL NOT BE INTERRUPTED."

He pointed a long finger at Holly Rash. "YOU. YOU WILL REPORT TO MY OFFICE IMMEDIATELY AFTER THIS ASSEMBLY. DO YOU UNDERSTAND?"

"Yes, but—"

"SIT DOWN."

Stunned, Holly got back in her seat.

"Tomorrow is not Pajama Day. It is not Rodeo Day. It is not Ugly Sweater Day. Tomorrow is, however, a very special theme day. Would you like to know what day tomorrow is?"

The room was silent.

"Tomorrow is School Day. And here is what you do on School Day: You put on clothes that conform to our dress code, you arrive to this campus *on time*, and you learn. And here is the good news: Today is also School Day. And so is next Monday. In fact, there are 120 School Days remaining this year, and all of them will be the same. You will learn facts, you will learn figures, you will be quizzed, and you will be tested. We will proceed thusly until June, at which point I do not care what you do. Wear a cowboy hat, wear a hideous sweater. That's what summer is for."

"WHY would we wear A SWEATER in SUMMER?" Stuart whispered to Scotty.

"YOU. IN THE THIRD ROW. YOU WILL REPORT TO MY OFFICE AS WELL."

"HOW the HECK did he HEAR ME?" Stuart said. (Principal Barkin heard him because Stuart was not great at whispering.)

"Now." Principal Barkin picked up his coffee mug. "We will talk about pranking."

Miles and Niles sat up straight.

"I am here in large part due to my predecessor's permissive attitude toward pranking. Let me tell you this: Although I may be related to your former principal, in that I am his father, I WILL NOT PERMIT PRANKS. School is about order. Humans have spent centuries classifying and codifying, organizing the world's information into a coherent system, and it is our job as educators to inscribe this system into your minds. We do not have time for pajamas, or pep rallies, or interruptions. We certainly do not have time for chaos."

He raised the mug to his mouth. It hovered before his lips, inches from his face.

"WE DO NOT HAVE TIME FOR PRANKS."

Bertrand Barkin drank deeply.

The Terrible Two leaned forward.

"OK," Niles whispered. (It was a good whisper.)

The principal's head snapped up.

His eyes widened.

Then he lifted his mug and took another sip. A long, slow sip. Bertrand Barkin looked out at the crowd as he sipped his coffee, and when he was done, he gave a satisfied sigh, right into the microphone.

"What?" whispered Miles.

Principal Barkin wore a thin smile.

"And so," said Principal Barkin, "there will be no pranks. Starting today, Yawnee Valley Science and Letters Academy is now a prank-free environment. This is something in which we will all take pride. It is something we will celebrate. It is something we will commemorate. Gus!"

Gus wheeled out a large object covered by a blanket.

"Today this sign will be hung in the front hall of Yawnee Valley Science and Letters Academy, right next to that ridiculous and misshapen cow."

Miss S., the first-grade teacher, frowned.

Bertrand Barkin whipped off the blanket.

"At the end of the day, I look forward to turning over number one. Furthermore, I fully expect we will continue turning over numbers, every day, until the end of the year.

"Now, children, you should know that I am not a man allergic to fun. When we make it to the last day of school without a single prank, that sign will reach 119. And to celebrate our good behavior, our reformation, we will have a treat: Sammy the Safety Lobster will present an assembly on summer safety."

There was a lot of grumbling.

"SILENCE!"

The grumbling stopped.

"You are dismissed," said Bertrand Barkin.

The teachers, who looked almost as shocked as the students, stood up and signaled to their classes to rise. As everyone was leaving the auditorium, Principal Barkin leaned over to Gus. Barkin spoke softly, but he made sure the microphone picked up his voice.

"Gus," he said, "we need to do something about those flowers out front."

"But it's illegal to pick a field violet, sir."

"I didn't say anything about picking. Put a tarp over them. Block out the sun. Let them die."

YOU PUT THE PEPPER IN, right?" Niles asked.

"Yes! Of course I put the pepper in."

"I know you did. I know you did."

Miles and Niles were walking across the front lawn with the rest of the class. A quick look over at the marquee revealed that the Pajama Day announcement had already been taken down. In its place:

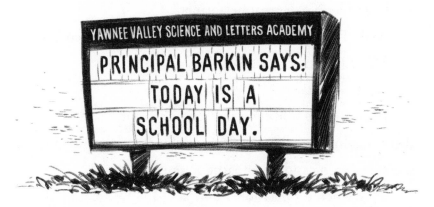

"That was the craziest thing I've ever seen," Miles said.

Niles just shook his head.

"He knew, right?" Miles said. "There's no way he wouldn't have tasted it. I mean, he knew."

"Yeah, he knew."

"I mean, he would have seen the pepper at the bottom of the mug."

"He knew."

"Man alive." Miles shuddered.

Holly caught up with them. "What's wrong? You guys look like you're the ones who got in trouble."

"Holly, be careful what you say in that office," Miles said. "That guy's a maniac."

Holly shrugged. "I'll survive," she said. "Honestly, I'm more upset about Sammy the Safety Lobster. That guy came in kindergarten. Not a great performer."

"WAIT, are you talking about SAMMY?" asked Stuart. "THAT DUDE is HILARIOUS."

Holly sighed.

They crossed through the school's front door. Gus was there, moving the cow to make room for the new sign. He gave the kids a shrug and a sympathetic smile.

"Hey, where'd Niles go?" Holly asked.

"He—" Miles looked around. "I don't know."

"All right. Well, later gator." She tucked in her shirt. "Stuart, time to talk to Barkin."

"Aw MAN."

They headed down the hall toward the principal's office. But Niles Sparks had beaten them there.

"You again." Bertrand Barkin leaned back in his chair.

"Me again!" said Niles. He walked back behind the desk and stood next to the principal.

Principal Barkin frowned. "Why are you on my side of the desk? Moreover, why are you here?"

"Ah!" Niles said. "I should have explained before the assembly. I'm the School Helper! You can tell because I'm wearing this sash. It says SCHOOL HELPER."

"I can read," said Principal Barkin. "And yet I have no idea what you're talking about." He looked at his watch. "What is this all about? I have students waiting outside to be disciplined."

"Excellent!" said Niles. "In that case, I'll be brief. The School Helper is a position I created, to help the school run well."

"And why," said Principal Barkin, "would I need help running the school?"

"Even Zeus had Hermes!"

Barkin scowled.

"Zeus," said Niles, "the Greek god."

"I'm familiar with Zeus," said Principal Barkin.

"Well, Hermes was—"

"I'm familiar with Hermes."

"Well, you're Zeus! And I'm Hermes! I can be your eyes and ears in the school. And your hands and feet too! You know, watching to make sure rules are followed. Listening for whispers of pranks. Enforcing your will."

"What about hands and feet?"

"Sorry?" said Niles.

"You said you'd be my hands and feet."

"*Enforcing.* That's hands."

"And feet?"

"Well." Niles's smiled faltered. "Walking. In places where you're not."

Barkin just stared.

"Think of me as a miniature Principal Barkin!" he said.

"It's a good idea," said Principal Barkin.

Niles exhaled. He'd been worried for a second. Now he'd have access to Old Man Barkin's office, his plans, his schemes—

"Give me that sash," said Principal Barkin.

"What?"

"Your sash. I'm relieving you of your position."

"But you just said it was a good idea!"

"It is. That doesn't mean I want *you* to be my School Helper. I'll be frank, Niles. I don't know you. I certainly don't trust you. And I don't think I like you."

"But—"

"Your sash."

Niles removed his sash. "But I made this myself."

Barkin took it. "And a fine job you did too. It should go well with Josh's eyes. They're Barkin brown."

"Josh?"

"Josh Barkin. My grandson. And new School Helper."

"You can't—"

"You're dismissed. Please send Holly Rash in."

Principal Barkin took a bite of the apple Niles had given him that morning. The apple was crisp, and the bite was loud.

Project 4 - Scented Candles

MILES AND NILES were in the prank lab. It was the following Sunday, and they were in the middle of an urgent planning session. The walls were covered in sketches, diagrams, and lists—a list of possible pranks (this list was long), a list of great pizza toppings (this list was even longer), a list of Old Man Barkin's weaknesses (there was nothing on this list).

"The problem with the pepper"—Miles had his mouth full of jelly beans—"is that Barkin knows we pranked him, but nobody else does."

"Right," said Niles. He was lying on the floor with his legs up so far against the wall that he was almost upside down.

"I mean, does he eat a lot of spicy foods? Or, and this is a scary thought, has he, like, trained his mouth to handle heat? Like, is he making himself prank-proof?"

"Maybe it's just mind over body," Niles said.

"It's tough," said Miles. "I mean, let's say we replace one of his power speeches with blank pieces of paper . . . Wouldn't work. He'd just make up some amazing speech on the spot. And nobody would ever know."

"Yeah," said Niles.

"Or we put a tack on his chair. Well, nope. I mean, he probably has spent his whole life developing super-strong butt muscles that repel sharp objects. He'd just sit there and smile."

"If you prank someone and nobody knows it, is it even a prank?" Niles asked.

Miles squinted at Niles. "You should probably stop lying like that. I think the blood's all rushing to your head."

"Wouldn't that be a good thing?" said Niles.

"What?"

"Well, then my brain would be getting more blood. More nutrients and oxygen."

"Fine." Miles was pacing. "What does your well-fed brain think we should do next?"

Niles just lay there, legs up.

"Niles," said Miles.

"Niles."

"Niles!"

"What?"

"What are you thinking about?"

"That sign."

"What sign?"

This sign:

On Thursday, after school, he'd watched Principal Barkin flip a bold black "1" down, covering up the rightmost zero. The pepper prank, a prank Niles was quite proud of, had been obliterated from Yawnee Valley history.

"The sign in the hall. The prank sign."

"OK, well, I'm trying to talk about Principal Barkin."

"The sign *is* Principal Barkin."

Part of being friends with Niles Sparks was sometimes having no idea what he was talking about.

"I have no idea what you're talking about."

"It's not just a sign. It's an instrument of power. A Doomsday Clock. Every time he flips over a number, the closer we get to eschaton."

"Eschaton?"

"Armageddon. Catastrophe. The end. Barkin wins. We lose."

Niles was making an odd expression—his eyes were unfocused while he chewed at his lip. Miles stared at his friend. He'd never seen Niles make this face before this last week, and now it was happening all the time. When had it started? When Old Man Barkin had taken Niles's sash? After Barkin swallowed the pepper coffee? Or even earlier, in the library, after Barry Barkin had been fired?

"Niles," said Miles. "Listen. If what you're saying is true, then maybe we don't need to prank Principal Barkin to beat Principal Barkin. We just need to stop the sign. Right?"

Niles's eyes snapped back into focus. "Right."

"So let's do something we know we're good at," said Miles. "My friend, I believe we've been looking at the wrong Barkin."

Niles flipped his feet over his head and turned to face Miles.

Miles smiled. "Let's prank Josh."

PRANKING JOSH BARKIN was practically an official pastime for the Terrible Two. Miles and Niles had it down to an art form. And today's exercise would be particularly elegant. Did you know you can pull a beautiful prank using only items from a sack lunch?

It was late autumn. The day was clear and cold. Miles and Niles, bundled up in coats, ate lunch on a bench far from the other kids. Miles gave Niles his apple bar and Niles gave Miles his fruit snacks, as usual. Unusually, they did not split Miles's Twinkie. They ate fast, packed up, and snuck into the locker room.

The locker room was cold—the locker room was always cold—and it smelled of chlorine, mildew, and the cologne some older boys used. The floor was gray. The lockers were gray. The lights were off and the whole room was gray.

The thick rubber mats on the ground dampened the noise from the Terrible Two's footsteps. The only sound was the dripping of a leaky showerhead. Here was locker #667, which belonged to Josh Barkin.

"All right," said Miles, running his hand against the cool metal. "Open it up."

Niles removed an empty soda can from his lunch bag, and Miles handed him a pair of scissors.

"Are you sure this works?" Miles asked.

Niles didn't answer. He sheared off the can's top and bottom, slit its side, and unfurled the aluminum on the ground. Working quickly, he cut out the shape of an M.

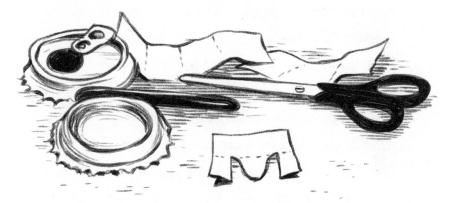

Then he folded the top half of the M down over itself.

And he folded the outside legs of the M up.

Niles held up the shim.

"Here it is," he said.

"It looks like underwear," said Miles.

"Like robot underwear," said Niles.

"Really skimpy robot underwear," said Miles.

They laughed for a few seconds before the mission continued.

Niles curved the shim around the U-shaped shackle of Josh's combination lock. He forced the metal down into the mechanism, wiggled it around a little, and—*click*—the lock popped open.

"Ha, ha!" Miles said. (He actually said, "Ha, ha!")

Miles grimaced and pushed Josh's gym clothes aside. Beneath a pair of ratty gray shorts was the prize they'd been seeking: a pair of blue sneakers with non-marking soles.

Niles unwrapped the Twinkie and broke it in half.

"Let us remember the noble sacrifice of this perfectly edible snack cake," he said, handing Miles a piece.

They dipped their fingers into the Twinkie's white cream and smeared the grease all over the bottoms of Josh Barkin's shoes.

In P.E. the prank went down like this:

Josh was the last one to change, as usual (he spent most of his time in the locker room throwing wet paper towels at a big mirror on the wall).

Coach B. started blowing his whistle at 2:09.

"One minute!" Coach O. shouted. "One minute and you're late."

Coach B. continued blowing his whistle every ten seconds as the stragglers poured forth from the locker rooms. Groups of girls rolling up the sleeves on their T-shirts, a boy who forgot his gym clothes skulking in jeans, slouching kids carrying novels.

"Ten seconds!" said Coach O.

Coach B.'s whistle-blowing had become frantic, and Coach O. waved a pack of pink slips in the air dramatically.

In the locker room, Josh heard the warning. He slicked back his hair in the mirror.

"Five!" said Coach O. "Four!"

Josh liked to cut it close, but he was a Barkin—he had a perfect attendance record to maintain. And so he shook the water off his hands and jogged across the locker room's rubber mat.

"Three!" said Coach O.

Josh crossed the trophy room's carpet.

"Two!" said Coach O.

Josh Barkin pushed open the big doors, jumped onto the gym's wooden floor, slid six feet, flapped his arms like a startled chicken, kicked one leg in the air, and fell over next to the volleyballs.

Coach B. stopped blowing his whistle.

Josh turned fuchsia.

The kids laughed loudly and the sound bounced all around the gym.

Coach O. grinned. "Ladies and gentlemen, Mr. Buster Keaton!"

Nobody laughed at that joke, but they were still laughing at Josh.

"The silent-film actor?" said Coach O. "He was always falling down? Come on, that's funny! I can't believe none of you know who Buster Keaton is!"

"I know who he is," said Holly.

"That was funny, right?" said Coach O.

"It was kind of funny," said Holly.

Meanwhile, Josh was on the ground, feeling the soles of his shoes.

"They're slippery!" he shouted. "My shoes are slippery!"

If he thought this revelation would make the kids stop laughing, he was wrong. They laughed harder.

Josh licked one of his fingers.

"Cream!" he said. "Somebody put cream on my shoes!"

"That's DISGUSTING!" said Stuart. "It's like you just LICKED your SHOE!"

"Shut up, nimbus!" Josh shouted. "I've been pranked!"

Miles and Niles looked at each other and scratched their

temples with two fingers. It was the way they gave their secret handshake when they wanted to keep it very secret.

Josh pointed the finger he'd just licked at the crowd. "Somebody pranked me!"

"NONSENSE."

A door opened. The laughter stopped. Everyone turned toward the back of the gym. Bertrand Barkin stood there in a dark suit.

"But—"

"SILENCE, JOSH," said Principal Barkin. "You're embarrassing yourself. I could hear your yowling from halfway across the lawn."

His shoes squeaked as he slowly made his way forward. He left a trail of black scuff marks behind.

Coach O. grimaced. This would mean hours of scrubbing on his hands and knees. "Principal Barkin," he said, "would you mind taking off your shoes? We just refinished these floors."

Bertrand Barkin froze. He stared at Coach O. "Did you just ask me to *take off my shoes?*"

"Yes, sir. We have a strict non-marking-sole policy in this gymnasium."

"Coach Orville," said Principal Barkin. He started walking again, and squeaking again, and the scuffs he left behind now were bigger and darker than the ones he'd been making before. "Do you really think that a principal would allow himself to be glimpsed at his school in *sock feet?* There is power in presentation." He stopped in front of Coach O. "An underdressed principal is like a coach without his whistle."

Bertrand Barkin gave the whistle around Coach O.'s neck a sharp tug. The nylon cord snapped.

"Powerless." The principal placed the whistle in his pocket. Coach O. swallowed and looked embarrassed.

"Now, Josh," said Bertrand. "What's all this hullabaloo?"

"Someone pranked me," Josh said. "We have to find them. We have to punish them."

Principal Barkin forced his thin lips into a thin smile.

"Don't be silly, Josh. Nobody pranked you. Students know better than to prank at this school."

"No, someone did, Grandfather."

"You will call me Principal Barkin at school, Josh."

"Someone did, Principal Barkin. They greased up the bottoms of my shoes."

"Nonsense. You are clumsy, and you fell."

"No! There's cream on my shoes!"

"You are clumsy. You fell."

"But feel them! They're all slippery."

"Josh, I am not going to touch your shoes. That is disgusting, and besides, there is no need. It's clear what happened here. You are clumsy. You fell."

"But this is a prank!"

Principal Barkin bent over his grandson, who still lay on the ground. His whisper came out as a hiss. "It is only a prank if we react. And we do not want pranks at this school. Do you understand me, boy?"

Josh nodded.

"Good. You are clumsy. You fell."

Josh nodded.

Principal Barkin straightened. "Tell everyone," he said.

"I am clumsy. I fell."

The gym was so quiet you could hear the dripping shower all the way in the boys' locker room.

Principal Barkin laughed. "It's true, I'm afraid. You *are* clumsy. Must come from your mother's side. Well, a fall in P.E. is nothing to make a fuss about. Shall we get this class started, coaches?"

And with that, Principal Barkin left.

"He still has my whistle," said Coach O.

"Here, borrow mine," said Coach B.

Josh picked himself up and stared at the class, who mostly stared at the ground. Not Niles, though. His gaze was far off, focused on nothing. It was that odd expression again.

Project 9 - Model Making

IN MS. SHANDY'S social studies class, Josh was eating a bag of chips.

"Josh," said Ms. Shandy, "you can't eat chips in class."

"Actually," said Josh, "I *have* to eat chips. It's for my blood sugar."

He licked orange dust from his fingers, one by one. Then he crinkled up the bag, stuffed it in his pocket, and pulled out a pudding cup.

"Josh," said Ms. Shandy.

"Ms. Shandy," said Josh, "if I don't eat this pudding cup, I could faint."

"Put it away, Josh," said Ms. Shandy.

"But I'm the School Helper!" said Josh.

"And I don't care," said Ms. Shandy.

"This position has power now! It's not like when he"—Josh nodded toward Niles— "was doing it."

"Three," said Ms. Shandy, "two—"

"But where am I supposed to put an open pudding cup?"

"Not my problem. One."

Josh gently set the pudding cup inside his backpack.

"And take off that hat."

Josh removed his cadet cap and fluffed up his hair.

"OK." Ms. Shandy turned back to the whiteboard, on which she had written two words in tall letters: "PROPAGANDA" and "SAMIZDAT."

"Now," said Ms. Shandy, "we discussed propaganda yesterday. Who can tell me what it is?"

Several kids raised their hands.

"Niles."

Niles made a big show of not reading from his notes: "Propaganda is the dissemination of doctrines and political ideas through art and culture."

"Good, Niles," said Ms. Shandy. "Propaganda can take the form of a movie, a book, or a play. A song, a painting, or a poster. But whereas art is an attempt to uncover the truth, propaganda promotes a party line, it maintains order, it instills in us those ideas that people want us to believe."

Niles wrote all this down.

"So," said Ms. Shandy. "Samizdat." She smiled at the class. "What the heck is that?"

Students chuckled.

"Nobody? Any guesses? Where do you think the word comes from? Holly?"

"It looks Russian?"

"That's right," said Ms. Shandy. "Samizdat comes from the Soviet Union. It means 'self-publishing.' Russian writers, intellectuals, and dissidents used to secretly make and pass around literature that the government, the state, wouldn't allow."

"It sort of sounds like SALAMI DOTS," said Stuart. "Like those WHITE DOTS in SALAMI!"

"Well," said Ms. Shandy, "samizdat often contained ideas that challenged authority, so the authorities made this writing illegal."

"Like me and my chips," said Josh.

"No, Josh," said Ms. Shandy. "The reason you can't eat chips in class is because it's distracting to students, and to me, and because you get orange dust all over your assignments, which is disgusting. The Soviet state believed samizdat was a threat to its very existence. Sorry, Josh, but your chips aren't that important."

"Disagree," said Josh.

Ms. Shandy went over to her desk and pulled out a pamphlet. The cover was gray and adorned with strange letters. "This is an actual piece of samizdat, a book of poems by a writer named Alexei Khvostenko." She handed it to Holly. "You can carefully pass that around. Josh, if you want to hold it, go wash your hands."

"That's it?" Josh asked, standing up to look at the book. "That's so flimsy."

"Samizdatchiks had limited resources—remember, they had to print these books themselves and smuggle them to readers. Samizdat is about the ideas inside, or really even about the idea of samizdat itself."

Holly passed the book to Niles, who carefully examined each page, even though he couldn't read it.

Ms. Shandy continued. "A lot of samizdat wasn't even political writing. But just the very fact that it existed, that rebels were making these books, that people could engage in this activity forbidden by the state—that was a threat to power."

"Cool," said Holly.

"And now," said Ms. Shandy, "I'd like everyone to get into their work groups."

The room was filled with metallic squeals as students scooted their chairs and rearranged their desks into groups of three.

"We're going to once again imagine that this classroom is organized by a system of government," said Ms. Shandy. This was one of her favorite exercises. Already this year, Room 22 had been a direct democracy, a theocracy, a republic, and an oligarchy.

"For the next two days," said Ms. Shandy, "we will be living in a totalitarian state."

"Sweet," said Josh.

"Now you will need to decide in your groups whether you are going to be propagandists or samizdatchiks. And you will be making either a propaganda poster or a piece of samizdat. So figure it out: Will you be the ruling party, or the underground?"

"Ruling party!" Josh Barkin told his groupmates, Janice Neeser and Stuart.

"I sort of thought it would be fun to make samizdat," said Janice Neeser.

Josh shook his head. "No way, nimbuses, we're the ruling party."

"Who made you president?" said Janice Neeser.

"I did," said Josh. He checked to see if Ms. Shandy was looking and put his cap back on. "I'm President Barkin and this is the ruling party."

"We RULE!" said Stuart.

Meanwhile, Holly was talking to Niles and Miles. "OK, I guess we should put this to a vote," she said. "I say samizdat."

"Samizdat," said Miles.

"Samizdat," said Niles.

"Really?" Holly looked at him, impressed. "I thought for sure you'd be a propagandist."

Ms. Shandy dinged a silver bell she kept on her desk.

"Listen up," she said. "By now you should have made your decisions. Here's the twist. Propagandists, you will have full access to the art supplies and the classroom computers. Samizdatchiks, you can use only these."

She held up a basket of old pencils. Many were chewed, and none had erasers.

Half the class groaned.

"Boom!" said Josh. "Told you, Janice. Power rules!"

"Now that you know the materials you're working with, it's time to decide what you're going to make. Plan carefully."

Ms. Shandy looked at the clock. "We have about fifteen minutes today, and you'll have some more time tomorrow."

Ms. Shandy walked around the room, absorbing the humming of students in conversation.

"What if we made a book of poems?" Holly said.

"I can't really write poems," said Miles.

"OK, then, like, a magazine?" said Holly.

Nearby, Josh was leaning back in his chair.

"Janice, you're good at drawing. Can you draw chips?"

"What?"

"Chips. I'm seeing a poster with a big bag of chips. And it says PRESIDENT BARKIN SEZ: IT'S A MEDICAL ISSUE. DON'T FAINT. EAT CHIPS. Do you know how to draw a doctor?"

"I guess," said Janice Neeser.

"And the doctor should have a chip for a head," said Josh.

"That's GENIUS," said Stuart.

After fifteen minutes, the bell rang. Backpacks zipped, three-ring binders clicked, and students marched out the door of Room 22.

When the room was empty, Principal Barkin marched in.

"Hello, Bertrand," said Ms. Shandy.

"Hello, Ms. Shandy," said Principal Barkin. "And may I remind you to address me as Principal Barkin."

"I thought that was just in front of students," said Ms. Shandy.

"It wasn't," said Principal Barkin. "Now. I hope you don't mind, but I was observing your class this morning through the window of the back door."

"I don't mind," said Ms. Shandy. "Although you were welcome to come in and observe."

Principal Barkin smiled. "I prefer to do my observations in secret. I find people change their behavior when they know I'm watching them."

"Right," said Ms. Shandy. She looked at the clock. By now there would be a line for the microwave in the teachers' lounge.

"I wanted to get a look at your teaching," said Principal Barkin. "But I didn't see any teaching."

"Excuse me?"

"From what I observed, you did a lot of walking around. While students chatted."

"We're working on a group project," said Ms. Shandy.

Principal Barkin made a face like he'd just bitten down on an olive pit. "A group project."

"That's right. They're learning from each other."

"Ms. Shandy," said Principal Barkin, "they're children. What do they have to teach each other?"

"Seriously? I believe that—"

"I was asking a rhetorical question," said Principal Barkin. "When I was a teacher, which I'll admit"—he gave an insincere chuckle—"was a long time ago, students learned from teachers. I held the knowledge, and I engraved it onto their soft minds."

"Times have changed," said Ms. Shandy.

"And now they're changing back," said Principal Barkin. "I witnessed pandemonium in here. And I will not have pandemonium in my classrooms!"

"Pandemonium?" said Ms. Shandy. She checked the clock again. "Listen, I have to go heat up my soup."

"Of course," said Principal Barkin. "I'm sorry to keep you. Go enjoy your lunch."

Ms. Shandy slung her tote over her shoulder and grabbed her keys. "Great talk," she said.

"Oh, this talk is not over," said Principal Barkin. "Please come visit my office during your prep period."

The next day Ms. Shandy lectured for the full forty-five minutes. There was no time devoted to group work. Propaganda and samizdat were never mentioned again.

Chapter 15

BACK IN THE PRANK LAB, a grim mood pervaded. A month had passed since the thwarted prank in the gym. That day, in big letters on the wall, Niles had written the words he'd heard Barkin whisper:

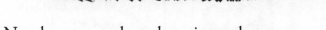

"IT IS ONLY A PRANK IF WE REACT."
— OLD MAN BARKIN

Now he sat cross-legged, staring at that sentence.

Miles was shelling a pistachio. "I've got an idea," he said.

"OK," said Niles.

"We need to go big."

"OK."

"I mean, we have to do something that is undeniably a prank."

"OK."

"And that's why"—here Miles tossed a pistachio into his mouth—"I propose a classic prank: We pull the fire alarm."

Niles said nothing.

"What do you think?" Miles asked.

Niles shrugged. "Feels a little pedestrian."

"Pedestrian?"

"Yeah, it's pretty obvious."

Miles's face flushed. "So what?"

"So what?" Niles asked. "It lacks panache. Where's the artistry, Miles? It just feels sort of . . . beneath us."

"You know," said Miles, "sometimes you can be real hard to be around."

"Come on, Miles," Niles said. "The fire alarm prank is in every movie, every TV show, every hokey comic book from the 1950s. It feels like the kind of thing you used to do before you came here."

"It *is* the kind of thing I used to do before I came here!" Miles didn't mention that when he did it at his old school, he was immediately caught and suspended for three days.

"I don't know," Niles said.

"Well, it's better than anything you've come up with. Better than sitting here staring at the wall, making that weird face."

Niles's voice was chilly. "I'm *thinking.*"

"Well, I'm trying to *do* something," Miles said. "Listen, I'm not saying it's a great prank. I'm not even saying it's a good prank. But obvious? That's the whole point! It's *obviously* a prank. It'll reset the Doomsday Clock! Isn't that what you want?"

Niles nodded. "Yes."

"Me too! And any other time, I'd say sure, let's cook up some great scheme. But we've got to stop Principal Barkin. Think about it. What does it say on that alarm? IN CASE OF EMERGENCY . . . PULL."

Niles chewed his thumbnail.

"So," said Miles. "Are you in or are you out?"

"Out," said Niles.

"Fine," said Miles.

MILES MURPHY PULLED the fire alarm on Monday afternoon. He did it on the way back from the bathroom, when the hallway was empty and nobody was looking. There was a little red lever, and when Miles pulled it, lights flashed, klaxons blasted, and sprinklers sprinkled. Miles smiled and let himself be drenched. Soon the hallway was filled with students—the younger kids walking hand in hand, two by two, the bigger kids moving in clumps. Teachers shouted. Doors swung. Kids laughed. Everybody got soaked. It was wonderful.

Miles found his class and sidled up to Niles.

Miles nodded.

Niles shook his head.

"THIS is CRAZY!" Stuart said. "IT'S like an INDOOR RAINSTORM!" He held open his mouth to catch some of the water.

"Gross, Stuart," said Holly. She sniffed the air. "I don't smell any smoke."

"THAT'S because THIS is a PRANK," said Stuart. "I can FEEL IT in my BONES."

"Somebody's going to pay," said Josh. "This is getting my sash all wet."

"Well, really it's my sash," said Niles. "I made it and—"

"QUIET! THIS IS AN EMERGENCY! YOU'RE SUPPOSED TO STAY QUIET DURING AN EMER-GENCY." Josh shook his head at Niles and wrote something down on the clipboard he was carrying.

"What are you writing?" Miles asked.

Josh shook his head at Miles and wrote something else on the clipboard.

"You can't even read it," Miles said, looking over Josh's shoulder. "The paper's all wet."

Josh underlined something on his clipboard. The pen tore through the sheet and his underline smeared into a big red blot.

Near the front office, they passed Gus, who was covering

the first-graders' cow with a tarp so the papier-mâché wouldn't get soggy. "You kids look like you went swimming!" he said, and waved.

♦ ♦ ♦

On the front lawn students gathered, grouped according to class. It was a gray day, with a breeze that raised goose bumps on Miles's wet skin and made him feel alive.

Teachers took roll. All students and staff were present and accounted for, except for one: Principal Barkin.

They waited.

The thrill of the interruption dissolved, and boredom crept over the crowd. Teachers stood holding first-aid kits, looking slightly lost. Miss S. led the first-graders in some sort of clapping game.

"I WISH we had a FRISBEE!" said Stuart. "KNOW what I MEAN?"

Nobody knew what he meant.

Then the front doors opened and a man in plaid emerged. It was Principal Barkin, dry as chalk dust beneath a black umbrella.

Bertrand Barkin strode over to the flagpole. He shook the water from his umbrella and collapsed it. "Children." He didn't need a megaphone to make himself heard. Barkin swung the umbrella, pointing its metal tip at the crowd.

"I will ask only once. Will the student who pulled the fire alarm please step up to the flagpole?"

"Oooooooooohhhhhh mamamamamamammaaaaaaa," said Stuart. "Somebody is in TROUBLE."

Kids looked around to see whether anyone was stepping forward. Miles scratched behind his ear and faked a yawn.

"A shame," Barkin said. "But unsurprising." He removed a medal from his pocket and dangled it before him. "I was looking forward to handing out this School Citizenship Award."

"WHAT?" said Stuart. "An AWARD? For a PRANK-STER?"

Miles frowned. This was odd. He looked at Niles, who stood still, staring, blinking.

"Prankster?" Principal Barkin looked at Stuart and smiled. "Oh, no, no. This award is for a hero."

"THIS is SO WEIRD," Stuart said. "KNOW what I MEAN?"

Everyone knew what he meant.

"Stuart, let's embrace this teachable moment," said Principal Barkin. "Pulling the fire alarm is a prank—and a rather crude prank at that—only when there is no fire."

"BUT there WASN'T a FIRE!"

Bertrand Barkin looked perplexed. "Of course there was, Stuart," he said. "There was a fire. Luckily, it was contained. The only thing lost was that wonderful papier-mâché mascot the first-graders made for our entrance. Burnt to a crisp. Most unfortunate."

Miles's throat tightened. "But we just saw that cow. That cow was fine."

"All right, students," Principal Barkin said. "Back to class. Today's a school day, after all."

He turned and slowly walked back toward the building.

When he reached the first step, he paused and removed a small box from his pocket. He turned it over in his fingers once or twice, then replaced it.

No way, thought Miles.

He must have seen that wrong.

"Are those MATCHES?" Stuart said.

"Man alive," said Miles.

When the kids went back to class, they walked by the charred remains of the Yawnee Valley Science and Letters Academy bovine. The burnt cow was still there at the end of the day, mostly just a pile of ash next to a sign that said:

YAWNEE VALLEY SCIENCE AND LETTERS ACADEMY

IT HAS BEEN
0 2 3 SCHOOL DAYS
SINCE OUR LAST PRANK.

Project 11 — Hand Turkeys

YAWNEE VALLEY SCIENCE AND LETTERS ACADEMY

IT HAS BEEN 0 4 2 SCHOOL DAYS SINCE OUR LAST PRANK.

AFTER THE FIRE, Bertrand Barkin got a new nickname. The students of Yawnee Valley Science and Letters Academy were divided into two groups. Most thought Barkin had heroically extinguished the blaze single-handedly. Some believed (but couldn't prove) that he set the fire himself. It didn't matter what side you were on: Now pretty much everyone called Barkin "Principal Invincible."

"Don't call him that," said Holly.

She was sitting behind a table of cakes. Cupcakes, carrot cakes, coffee cakes and tea cakes, pound cakes, Bundt cakes, crumb cakes and sponge cakes, angel food cakes, devil's food cakes, strawberry shortcakes and pineapple upside-down cakes. Red velvet. Tres leches. Whoopie pies. It was a bake sale.

To Holly's right was a metal cash box. To her left was an open book of poetry, one that was not assigned schoolwork. She read from the book when the bake sale was slow.

Stuart was at the front of the line. Scotty was right behind him, impatiently eyeing the flan. Miles and Niles were off to the table's side, hanging out near Holly, which was something they often did at lunch. When things got busy, they offered help Holly didn't need. Otherwise they sat there while she read.

"Don't call him WHAT?" said Stuart.

"Principal Invincible."

"But EVERYONE calls him that."

"I don't," said Holly.

"Neither do I," said Niles.

"Me neither," said Miles.

BAKE SALE
FUNDING THE Y.V.S.L.I.
STUDENT-PARENT DINNER-music talking
DANCE. ☆FEATURING☆ dancing spaghetti.

"Why NOT?" said Stuart. "It RHYMES!"

Holly shook her head. "Nobody is invincible."

"What if he IS, though?" Stuart said. "Like ONCE, I played this VIDEO GAME, and you had to fight this ONE BOSS, and he was INVINCIBLE. What if Principal Barkin is like THAT?"

"What video game?" Miles asked.

"Oh MAN," said Stuart. "I can't REMEMBER. But the BOSS was SO scary. It was this GIANT SPIDER, and it was covered in ARMOR, and your ARROWS couldn't PIERCE the armor, and it released TINY SPIDERS from its MOUTH. It was NUTSO!"

Miles bit into a madeleine. "Did the spider have eyes?"

"It had SO many EYES!"

"Did the eyes flash?"

"YEAH! Right before it SPAT the TINY SPIDERS!"

"You have to shoot the eyes when they flash."

"OH." Stuart pounded his forehead. "I didn't even TRY that."

"See," said Holly. "Nobody's invincible."

"I GUESS."

"Stuart's right, though," Niles said. "I am surprised Principal Barkin hasn't canceled the dance."

Holly shut her book, allowing Niles to glimpse the cover. *Collected Poems of Emily Dickinson.*

"Think about it, guys," said Holly. "This dance is a tradition. Barkin's great-grandfather held the first dance in 1894, and there's been one every year since."

Miles and Niles nodded.

Holly grinned. "Everyone has a weakness. And what's Barkin's weakness? Tradition. Family honor. All that. So I'm going to exploit that weakness, and this school's going to get to do something fun."

"SORT OF fun," said Stuart.

"What?" said Holly.

"I MEAN, nobody LOVES the dance."

The Student-Parent Dinner-Dance was typically the least popular event hosted by the student council. That's because it was a dance, with parents. Also the dinner was bad. (It was always the same: soft spaghetti.) But it wasn't true that *nobody* loved the dance. The parents loved it.

"Why are you still here, Stuart?"

"Can I get my MONEY back? This CUPCAKE is really DRY."

"Hey, I made that cupcake!" Miles said.

Stuart looked at Miles. "Well, it's DRY."

"No refunds," said Holly. "You can exchange it for anything in this section."

Stuart grabbed a streusel and left.

"What does *he* know?" Holly said.

"Totally!" said Miles. "Like Stuart's suddenly Doctor Cupcake, and we're supposed to just trust him on how dry stuff is? No thank you."

"I meant about the dance," said Holly.

For Holly, throwing the dance had become enormously important. It was the only extracurricular event left on the school calendar. The Student-Parent Dinner-Dance was an affront to power, a glimmer in the dark, an arrow in the spider's eye.

Josh, clad in a khaki cap and Niles's sash, cut the line.

"Hey," said Scotty. "No cuts!"

Josh pointed at the sash. "School Helper. I don't have to follow the rules."

"Actually," said Niles, "the School Helper's job is to make sure the rules are always followed, and it's important to lead by example, so you should probably—"

"Shut up, nimbus," said Josh. "I'm not here to talk to you. Or this nimbus. Or this nimbus. I'm not here to talk. I'm here to pick up this money." Josh reached for the cash box.

Holly slammed down the lid and left her hand on top of it.

"What?" she asked.

"The money, nimbus."

"This is a student council fund-raiser. Which means this is student council money. And you're not on the student council."

"I'm commandeering the cash, nimbus. This money is being redirected to the School Helper Fund."

"But, Josh," said Niles, "School Helper is a volunteer position, and doing the job doesn't really cost any money, so—"

"Nimbus," said Josh, "the only reason I'm not handing you a detention right now is professional courtesy for a former School Helper."

"But School Helpers can't hand out detentions," said Niles.

"Now they can." Josh pulled out a pack of pink slips from his pocket. He fanned through them. "Boom."

Niles frowned.

"Anyways," said Josh, "I told you. I'm not here to talk. I should be helping the school. So, Holly, if you'll please hand over the money—"

"Not going to happen."

Josh grabbed the handle. So did Holly.

"Well," said Josh, "I guess we should take this matter to the principal, who is also my grandfather."

"I guess we should," said Holly.

With her free hand, Holly put up a sign that said BAKE SALE CLOSED—BACK SOON.

Holly and Josh marched down to Barkin's office, carrying the cash box between them.

"Darn," said Scotty. "I really wanted some flan."

Holly and Josh stood in front of Principal Barkin's desk. They'd each finished telling their side of the story.

"Josh," said Principal Barkin, "please leave."

Josh stood up and reached for the cash box.

"Leave the box, Josh," said Principal Barkin.

"But, Grandfather—"

Principal Barkin winced.

Josh tried again. "But, Principal Barkin—"

"You are dismissed."

Holly smirked at Josh while he made his exit.

Barkin reclined. He scratched his mustache. He smiled. "Holly," he said. "I'm glad you came to my office."

"Me too," said Holly. "And thank you, sir. I know Josh is your grandson, but that was ridiculous. He can't just go around taking student council money."

"Why, of course he can."

"*What?*"

"Of course he can. And I'm glad he did. Holly, it's my understanding that last year, on a technicality, you defeated my grandson in the race for school president. Am I correct?"

"Yes."

"Of course I am. I respect that, Holly. I always respect a power grab."

"I don't know if I'd call it a—"

"But you grabbed power from the wrong person. You grabbed power from a Barkin."

Principal Barkin leaned forward and rested his elbows on the desk.

"You have to understand, Holly. When a Barkin has been a

student at this school, he has been class president. That is a tradition, a tradition of power. It's a tradition you broke with your power grab. And although I respect a power grab, that doesn't mean I like it. And I certainly don't like the grabber. Am I being clear?"

"Yes and no," said Holly.

Barkin sneered. "You have a smart mouth, Holly Rash. And I don't like that, either. But let me give you a little lesson in power. Josh can take the student council's money whenever he wants to."

"That's stealing."

"No, that's commandeering. Do you know the difference between commandeering and stealing? When the powerless take, it's stealing. When the powerful take, it's commandeering."

"But I'm the class president," Holly said.

"Yes. And Josh is the School Helper."

"But that's just some dumb job Niles made up a few years ago."

"That may be so. But I've reorganized the power chart. Do you know what a power chart is, Holly? It's a diagram that describes the flow of power through a school. Here is the power chart when School Helper was, as you say, just some dumb job."

Principal Barkin drew on a legal pad.

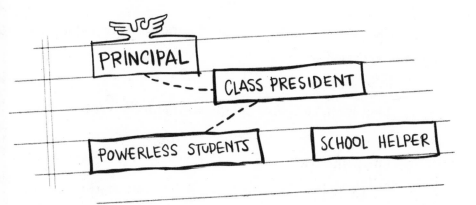

Barkin tore off the page and started again. "But look at this!"

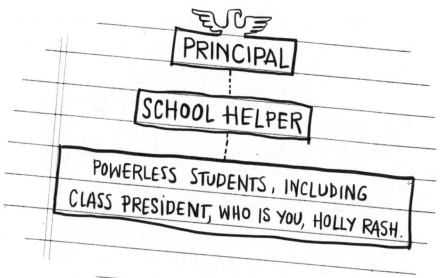

"But you can't just redraw a chart and change the way the whole school works," Holly said.

"Of course I can," said Principal Barkin. "Who is at the top of both charts?"

Holly sighed.

"That wasn't a rhetorical question, Holly. Who is at the top?"

"The principal."

"That's right. The principal. All power at this school flows from the principal, including the power to draw power charts. And now that School Helper is such a powerful position, we've needed to create a School Helper Fund, which will allow Josh to better enforce school rules. We're in something of a state of emergency here, Holly, in case you haven't noticed. Before I came, rules were being broken willy-nilly. It was havoc. And I must restore order. That takes money."

"But these are funds for the Student-Parent Dinner-Dance."

Barkin leaned farther forward. He was more than half-way across his desk.

"Yes," he said. "The Student-Parent Dinner-Dance. A silly tradition, and one that has outlived its usefulness. I would have canceled it, but parents love it. And in a time of emergency, I can't spend all day fielding phone calls from angry parents telling me how to run my school. Parents do not run a school. The principal runs a school. Unfortunately, many parents don't understand that, and these are people to whom I loathe speaking. And so I thank you, Holly."

"Why?"

"Because. The cancellation of this year's dinner-dance is not on my hands. It's on yours."

Holly took a few steps back.

"How does this sound?" said Barkin, leaning forward even more. "I'm afraid that the student council failed to raise the funds necessary to hold the dance. Sad, really. And with budget cuts, blah, blah, blah. You get the idea. Now, please take this cash box to the cafeteria and hand it over to my grandson. You are dismissed."

By the time Holly returned to the bake sale table, a long line had formed. Josh was plumping himself up at the front, shining one of his medals with his shirtsleeve.

"Hello, Holly," he said.

She handed over the box. "Here."

"Thank you, Madam President," said Josh. He got behind the table and took down the poster Holly had made the night before. "Now," he said, "who wants some cake? Proceeds help me help the school."

Scotty stepped up and selected a flan.

"Scotty," said Holly, "don't. That money's just going to go to Josh."

Scotty shrugged. "I'll pay whoever has the flan."

Holly slumped against the wall.

"What happened in there?" Niles asked.

Holly said, "Principal Invincible canceled the dance."

Project 15 - Quilting

Chapter
18

THE COUNT ON OLD MAN BARKIN'S sign grew higher: 50, then 60, then 70. The Terrible Two took tests. They passed quizzes. They read about the gold rush and metonymy and complementary angles. When the covers on their textbooks tore, they made new ones by cutting up brown paper grocery bags. They watched a movie version of _Romeo and Juliet,_ but Mr. Gebott fast-forwarded through a bunch of it. They had indoor recess for two consecutive weeks. They found patterns in the bubbles they filled out on answer sheets (the reading section of the state test had five _E_s in a row). They gave valentines to every kid in their homeroom, even though Niles wanted to send only one and Miles would have rather not sent any. They wore green on St. Patrick's Day but still got pinched by Josh Barkin. The Terrible Two did all these things. What they did not do was prank.

For days, for weeks, for months, everything went exactly as everyone expected. There were no surprises. It had been 81 school days since the last prank.

One Saturday, Miles and Niles were not in the prank lab. They were in the driveway in front of Miles's house, sitting on skateboards. By shifting their hips, they could make the skateboards roll back and forth, and for an hour they'd been swaying like buoys on the pavement.

They'd been doing that a lot these days.

"You know what Wednesday is?" Miles asked.

Niles knew what Wednesday was. Miles knew what Wednesday was. Ms. Shandy had a giant calendar on a bulletin board in her classroom, and they'd been watching it coming for three weeks now. Ms. Shandy's calendar marked due dates for research papers, test days, holidays. All through March, Miles and Niles had been looking toward the end of the month, and the beginning of the next.

April 1.

April Fools' Day.

The official holiday of pranksters, Feast Day of the International Order of Disorder, and the one-year anniversary of the first prank ever pulled by the Terrible Two, which was also the greatest prank Yawnee Valley had ever seen.

"It's April Fools' Day," said Miles.

"I know," said Niles.

"So," said Miles.

"So," said Niles.

They swayed back and forth.

"Got any ideas?" Miles asked.

"Honestly? I haven't really been thinking about it."

It was terrifying to hear those words come out of Niles's mouth.

The truth was, Miles hadn't really been thinking about it either—lately he'd been lacking inspiration. But he'd comforted himself by imagining that Niles's brain had continued to buzz and hum, planning, theorizing, philosophizing. When he saw Niles making his weird faraway look, Miles was sure he was cooking up pranks. Or at least he had hoped Niles was. But now he knew. And the knowledge that Niles's head had been as empty as his own these past few months filled Miles with a retroactive dread.

The wheels of the skateboards grumbled as they ground up loose gravel.

"Can I ask you a question?" Miles asked.

"OK," said Niles.

It was something Miles had been wondering for a long time.

"Were you a prankster first, or a kiss-up?"

Niles stopped moving.

"A kiss-up."

Miles nodded.

"I mean," said Niles, "I guess I was sort of a born kiss-up. My mom and dad were both kiss-ups, or I think *you* would have probably called them kiss-ups. They're both really smart. Like, *really* smart. And so they always expected me to be really smart. And when I *was* really smart, it was just sort of like, yep, that's how it's supposed to be. When I bring home my report card, they just smile and nod."

"Man," said Miles. "When I get more than three As, my mom takes me out for ice cream."

"Yeah," said Niles.

"Sometimes it seems like she feels bad about it. She says, 'I shouldn't be bribing you to do well in school.' But we go anyway. Part of it is I think she just really likes ice cream. Still, the one time I got straight As she went nuts. I got to pick what we had for dinner for a week. It was weird—when I went to her work, the other people there were congratulating me, so I could tell she'd been talking about it to pretty much *everybody*."

"Yeah."

"Sorry," said Miles. "That's probably not helping."

"No, it's OK. I'm fine about it."

They sat some more.

"But my parents aren't really like that," Niles said. "If I messed up, it was a national crisis. But if I did something good, nobody really cared. It was just the way the world was supposed to be—everything in the right order. So I tried to do better and better—safety patrol, volunteering, School Helper—all that stuff. But . . ."

"No ice cream."

"No ice cream."

"Well," said Miles, "when my mom feels bad about bribing me, she always says excellence should be its own reward."

"Yeah, I don't really believe that."

"Yeah, me neither."

"I mean," said Niles, "it seems like excellence should get you *something*. But I was just this weird kid who wore a suit and a sash and didn't have any friends."

"That's definitely what I thought when I first met you."

"I've always loved books," Niles said. "And my favorite books were books about pranksters. And books about how to do pranks. And how to make secret codes, and how to sneak around. From the time I was really little, I was always dreaming up pranks. I used to sit on my bed and imagine how I'd booby-trap my room. When I was six I asked for a bucket for Christmas, so I could fill it up with water and hook up a trip wire so it would spill on whoever came into my room."

Miles smiled. "Such a classic."

"Yeah. But nobody really ever came to my room."

"Oh," said Miles. "Right."

"It's OK," said Niles. "I was too afraid to set it up anyway. I never really did any pranks. I just thought about them all the time. I was afraid if I ever actually pulled a prank, I'd get in huge trouble. But then I realized: All those years of ex-cellence *had* gotten me something. They'd gotten me lots of things: complete access to the school, the trust of Principal Barkin, and total cover. I was above suspicion."

"Right!" said Miles.

"I was perfectly positioned to pull all those pranks I'd been thinking of for years. So last year I decided I'd finally do it. And on the first day of school, I parked Barkin's car on the top of the stairs."

Miles fell off his skateboard on purpose. "What! Niles, that was your first prank?"

Niles smiled. "Yeah!"

Miles lay on his back and looked up at the sky. "Holy crow. Niles."

"What?"

"You're wrong, man."

"What do you mean?"

"Niles, you're not a born kiss-up. You're a born prankster."

"Yeah?"

"Yeah. And Niles." Miles turned and looked at his friend. "We have to keep pranking until we beat Barkin."

Eastern whip-poor-will

SCHOOL BUS

Common Yawnee Raccoon

mountain cottontail

• YAWNEE VALLEY SCIENCE •
TRACK AND FIELD • TRAC

White-tailed Deer

Project 18 - Nature Photography

Chapter

19

DURING MORNING BREAK on April 1, the Terrible Two stood in the basement of Yawnee Valley Science and Letters Academy. Miles had a lunch bag so heavy he held it from the bottom. Niles carried a small cage that once belonged to his hamster, which escaped and had vanished when he was in second grade.

In front of them was a large red door with peeling paint and block letters.

For now at least, the coast was clear. Miles had made a mixture of sour cream, raw eggs, and pea soup the night before—he'd brought it to school and poured it on the playground, by the swings, at the beginning of recess. Gus had emerged with a bag of sawdust and a broom. Phase One: Fake Vomit was complete. They had at least seven minutes before Gus returned. It was time to initiate Phase Two.

Niles produced an enormous ring from his pocket—the copied master set of keys was the crowning accomplishment of his stint as School Helper.

"They may take my sash, but they'll never take my keys," he said.

He began trying keys one by one, fitting each one into the lock and giving it a little wiggle.

Nope.

Nope.

Yep.

The mechanical room was vast and dusty. It smelled of oil. The air was old—it hung above them and tasted stale in their mouths. Nobody but Gus had breathed in here for the last thirty years. The room was still and mostly quiet. Occasionally there was a clang or a rumble. Two hot-water tanks towered like sentries by the door. Pipes of many sizes crisscrossed overhead. On the back wall, a row of circuits twinkled. In the middle of the room was a great metal block.

That was it.

The furnace.

The boys approached with something like reverence. The furnace was taller than they were and ran half the length of the room. Niles ran his hand against the metal and was surprised to find it was cool. Somewhere within this machine was an infernal blaze that pumped heat to the school's twenty-two classrooms.

Niles pulled out some diagrams he'd copied from a book at the library.

"OK," he said. "Well, I thought this would make more sense when we were in the room."

Miles looked over Niles's shoulder, then at the furnace. "I think it actually makes less sense now that we're in the room."

"Yeah," said Niles. "That might be true."

They stared at the diagrams for a few more seconds.

"Well," said Niles, "I guess we should look for this lever."

They slowly walked around the furnace in opposite directions.

"Hey!" said Miles. "Is this it?"

He was pointing at a recessed lever at the head of the machine. Niles checked it against the diagram. "Yeah! I think it is."

"You think?"

"I mean, it is."

"What if I pull this and the whole thing explodes?" said Miles.

"I don't think that's really how furnaces work," said Niles.

"Yeah," said Miles. "It would be cool, though."

Miles pulled down on the lever and an inspection panel swung open, revealing a wall of buttons, tubes, and wires. Niles could now hear a muffled roar. And through a little round window down near the ground, Niles could make out the flicker of an orange flame.

"All right," he said. "We're almost in. We just open that little panel and then it's go time."

"Ready the vessel," said Miles.

Niles put the hamster cage on the ground.

"Vessel is ready," said Niles. "Apply protective gear layer one."

They clipped wooden clothespins to their noses.

"Pour the cheese," said Niles.

"Pouring the cheese," said Miles.

He dumped four pounds of Limburger into the cage.

"Apply protective gear layer two."

The Terrible Two donned safety goggles and oven mitts.

"Let's go."

Niles pulled a small lever and a panel the size of an oven door swung open.

The roar of the furnace was loud now, and hot air

blasted their faces and blew back their hair. Niles studied the coils in front of him, which snaked up to a metal grate.

"That's it. The air handler."

Niles placed the cage on top of the grate.

He checked their handiwork against a drawing he'd made himself.

"We good?" Miles asked.

"We're good," Niles said.

The soft cheese had already begun to melt, running goopily on the cage's metal bottom.

It occurred to Niles that he had not yet smelled Limburger cheese. He removed his clothespin, just for a second.

It was worse than he thought.

The bell rang.

"Happy April Fools' Day," said Miles.

"Happy April Fools' Day," said Niles.

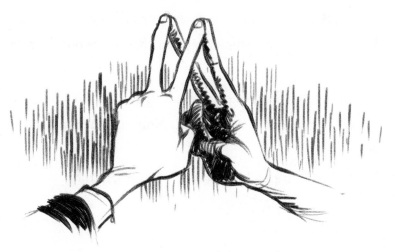

THE STENCH HIT IN MATH CLASS. At first it was faint—a pungent trace Niles could taste at the edges of each breath. He looked up from his worksheet and caught Miles's eye. Soon the funk was filling the classroom. The heat pouring in was fetid and moldy, aggressively moist. The scent searched out your nostrils and curled inside, burning your nose. Room 18 smelled of swamps and death. Which meant the whole school was filled with this evil air. Niles gagged. It was wonderful.

He waited for someone to say something.

The class continued to fill out their worksheets.

Many kids had covered their noses with sweatshirt sleeves. Some pinched their noses closed. But everyone kept doing math.

Niles looked at Miles, who shrugged and shook his head.

The whole room was putrid. Nobody reacted. How could this be?

"Stuart," Niles whispered, "do you smell that?"

"YEAH," whispered Stuart. "It smells like FEET."

"I bet you could think of a good foot joke to make right now."

"Right NOW? I'm doing a WORKSHEET right now."

"Holly," said Niles, "you smell that, right?"

"Yeah, of course. It's awful."

"I think it's pretty clear what's going on, right?"

"Yeah. A rat must have died in the ducts or something."

"No! Today's April first."

"OK..."

"It's probably an April Fools' prank!"

Holly turned to Niles. "Seriously? Last year, maybe. But not with Principal Invincible. People don't prank at this school anymore."

Niles was sweating. The scent was overwhelming.

"Scotty?" said Niles hopelessly.

"Niles!" said Ms. Knox. "Quiet down and finish your worksheet."

Niles's vision was blurring, and he didn't know whether it was the cheese or his desperation. Miles looked horrified.

"Thank you for your maturity, students," said Ms. Knox. "It seems something's wrong with the heater. I know it's cold outside, but Stuart, would you open the windows?"

"OK!" said Stuart.

"I'll call Principal Barkin and let him know," said Ms. Knox, "although I daresay he's already smelled this. I'm sure he'll put everything in order soon."

Stuart fiddled with a latch. The window squeaked. A cold blast of fresh air ran through the classroom.

"No!" yelled Niles.

"Niles Sparks!" said Ms. Knox. "What's gotten into you? You're not acting like yourself."

Niles wanted to stand up on his desk and shout, "I AM NILES SPARKS, ONE HALF OF THE TERRI-BLE TWO. IT IS APRIL FOOLS' DAY, YOU HAVE BEEN PRANKED, AND WE ARE THE ONES WHO PRANKED YOU. PUT DOWN YOUR PENCILS AND LOOK ALIVE."

But he didn't.

Instead he stayed in his seat and threw up.

NILES WENT HOME SICK. He was out for the rest of the week. Miles didn't know what happened. Niles wouldn't answer the phone. He wouldn't come to the door.

"Niles isn't feeling well" was all Niles's mom said when Miles biked to his house on Saturday. (Niles's mom was not too friendly.)

On Sunday, Miles tried again and got the same answer.

On Monday, Niles still didn't come to school.

During lunch, Miles sat alone on a bench and watched the other kids. There was nobody he wanted to eat with. He was so worried, he didn't even want to eat.

What had happened to his best friend? Had Niles snapped? Would he leave school forever? Was he going to transfer to St. Perpetua, or get homeschooled, or move to another town? And even if Niles did come back, would he stop pranking?

Had Principal Invincible broken Niles's spirit?

Was this the end of the Terrible Two?

Had the story of these two great pranksters come to an end?

No way, of course not. There are still thirty-eight pages left in this book.

After school, Miles found a rubber chicken in his locker.

Miles smiled.

(Rubber chickens with secret codes were the preferred method of communication between pranksters, or at least this is something Niles always said.)

He arrived at Niles's room at 3:42 p.m.

Niles was standing by the window.

"What are you wearing?" Miles asked.

"A toga!" said Niles. "I made it from a bedsheet!"

"Why?"

"Because," Niles said, "we're going to talk philosophy! The philosophy of pranking."

"Oh boy."

"Here." Niles picked up another sheet. "I made one for you too."

"I think I'll pass."

"But Miles! Ever since the founding days of the International Order of Disorder, pranksters have been meeting to discuss the fundamentals and ethics of pranking."

"Wearing togas?"

"Yes! The practice goes back to ancient times!"

Miles sighed and draped the sheet over his shoulders.

"Yours might feel a little funny," Niles said. "It's the fitted sheet."

Indeed, Miles had to fiddle with the elastic. "OK," he said.

"Great! Now here are your laurel leaves."

"Is this parsley?"

"Miles."

Miles donned the parsley.

"You look great," said Niles. "Now, let's have a dialogue."

"Isn't that what we've been doing?"

"Sure," said Niles. "But in a dialogue, you ask big questions."

"OK," said Miles. "What the heck are we listening to this time?"

"The music of Shakespeare's time, recorded on Elizabethan instruments," said Niles. "Bigger questions, Miles, ones whose answers aren't so obvious."

Miles rolled his eyes. "Fine. Where have you been all week?"

"Playing hooky," said Niles. "It's been great!"

"Why didn't you tell me?"

"Tell you what?"

"That you were fine."

"Oh. Yes. I didn't think of that. Maybe I should have."

"Maybe? Definitely."

"Why definitely?"

"Because! I could have helped you!"

"How?"

"By asking questions!"

"Questions like 'What the heck are we listening to?'"

"No! Big questions!"

"Miles," said Niles, "I needed time alone."

"Why?" said Miles.

"Because something has been bothering me."

"But I'm your friend," said Miles. "I could have helped you."

"Sometimes I need to be away from everybody," said Niles, "so I can walk around inside my brain. Besides, you already did help me. The thing that's been bothering me is a question you already asked me. A big question."

"What question?"

"I'll get to that later. Now it's my turn to ask questions. Miles, why did our April Fools' Day prank fail?"

"Because you threw up?"

"No! No. It failed before that."

"It failed because Stuart opened the window."

"But why did he open the window?"

"Because Ms. Knox told him to."

"And why did she tell him to?"

"Because the school smelled disgusting."

"So didn't we succeed? Wasn't that our goal: to make the school smell disgusting?"

"No," said Miles. "Our goal was to make everybody go nuts.

They should have started laughing. There should have been a riot. But they just sat there and did their worksheets."

"So," said Niles, "what could we have done better?"

Miles thought for a long time. He was disappointed with his answer. "I don't know," he said. "I don't think we could have done anything better."

"I agree," said Niles. "It was perfect."

"So why did it fail?" Miles asked.

"It wasn't the smell that made me throw up. It was what Holly said. Did you hear her? She said, 'People don't prank at this school anymore.'"

Miles nodded. "And there was a prank under everyone's noses. Literally."

"Miles," said Niles. "*We* prank at that school."

Niles opened the door to the prank lab. He picked up a piece of chalk.

"But if there's no reaction," said Miles, "there's no prank."

"Precisely. And if there are no pranks, there are no pranksters. And if there are no pranksters, you're just the new kid and I'm a weirdo in a sash."

"You don't even have the sash anymore."

Niles nodded grimly. "Well, I for one don't intend to go back to being just a weirdo. I'm a prankster."

"So what do we do?" Miles asked.

"Why didn't people react to our prank?"

"Because Old Man Barkin convinced them pranks don't happen."

"And why is Old Man Barkin our principal?"

"Because Original Barkin got fired."

"And why did he get fired?"

The Terrible Two looked at each other.

"Because of our prank," said Miles.

"Yes," said Niles. "Principal Barkin got fired because of our prank."

"But you said we couldn't have known Old Man Barkin was a skunk!" said Miles. "We couldn't have known he'd use our pranks to fire his own son! You said it wasn't our fault."

"Yeah," said Niles. "But I was wrong. It is our fault. We couldn't have known all that. But we know all that now. Miles, last November, when we heard Old Man Barkin yell at Principal Barkin on speakerphone, you asked me a question. A very big question. I didn't want to think about it then and I don't really want to think about it now. But I have been. You asked, 'Should we feel bad for Principal Barkin?' And the answer is, I feel terrible."

"Me too," said Miles.

"I feel like when you tell a joke about someone, and then it turns out they're right behind you. Only worse. Much worse. We didn't mean to, but I think our prank ruined Principal Barkin's life. And, Miles, we took an oath. An oath to never destroy."

"So what are you saying?" Miles asked.

"We need to fix this. We need to come up with a way to prank Old Man Barkin and get Original Barkin his job back. We need to put back together what we destroyed."

"So be it," said Miles.

"So be it," said Niles.

"But, Niles, here's another very big question. How do we prank Old Man Barkin?"

Niles smiled. "Turns out we answered that question months ago and didn't even know it."

He pointed to an empty list on the wall:

Miles frowned. "I don't get it."

"What's Old Man Barkin's greatest weakness?" Niles asked.

Miles shrugged. "He doesn't have any."

"Exactly."

"Exactly?"

"Exactly. His greatest weakness is that he doesn't have any weaknesses."

"Um, I'm pretty sure that's his greatest strength."

"It's both. He's made everybody think he's invincible. All we have to do is prove that he's not, and the whole thing will come crashing down on his head."

"OK," said Miles. "But how?"

Niles took a sprig of parsley from behind his ear and chewed on it. "We're going to need help."

Chapter 22

THE TERRIBLE TWO arrived at the home of Barry Barkin ten minutes later. They stashed their bikes in a hedge and rang the doorbell.

"You sure about this?" Miles asked.

"No," said Niles.

Josh Barkin answered the door.

"What do you two nimbuses want?"

"We need to talk to your dad," said Niles.

Josh narrowed his eyes. "Why?"

"None of your business," said Miles.

Josh shut the door in their faces.

Niles rang the doorbell again.

"Go away, nimbuses."

One more time.

Mrs. Barkin answered the door.

"Now, what is going on out here?" she asked.

"You must be Mrs. Barkin!" said Niles. "I recognize you from the pretty picture Principal Barkin used to keep on his desk. We're two of your husband's favorite students."

"Well, then you must be Niles Sparks!" said Mrs. Barkin. "I've heard so much about you." She turned to Miles. "And you are?"

"Miles Murphy," said Miles.

"Oh." Her smile faltered. "Yes. Well, I've heard a bit about you too."

Niles stepped in quickly. "We'd love to have a word with Mr. Barkin."

"Oh! Well, I'm sure he'd be delighted to see you both, especially you, Niles, but I'm afraid Barry isn't here right now. He's at the quarry, testing out his new hang glider."

"His what?" Miles asked.

"His hang glider. Barry's latest project. It's all projects with that man these days, projects, projects, projects. Suddenly it's hang gliding. He built it himself."

"He did?" asked Miles and Niles at the same time.

"Yes, named it and everything."

Miles and Niles exchanged a look.

They had to get over to the quarry.

The sun was low and purple in the west when the boys

arrived at the quarry. At the top of a hill, Niles spotted the silhouette of a figure with strange, batlike wings.

"Barkin," he said.

They pedaled up switchbacks and rode hard along a path that ran along the quarry's edge. To their right, the hill had been carved out—the gentle upslope ended abruptly in a sheer cliff that ran down into blackness. As they approached their former principal, they could see his hot breath in the evening air. He was strapped into the great contraption, fumbling with some buckles.

"CONFOUND YOU, YOU CLAPTRAP WHIRLI-GIG," Barkin said, apparently to the hang glider.

The wind gusted, picking up dust and leaves and whipping them into little whirlwinds.

"Principal Barkin!" Miles shouted.

It seemed Barkin couldn't hear them. Satisfied with whatever last-minute adjustments he was making, he stepped to the edge of the quarry. He completed a series of energetic deep knee bends, then straightened.

Niles rang his bike's bell.

Barkin cocked his head.

"Principal Barkin!" Miles and Niles shouted together.

He turned toward them and raised a gloved hand to his eyes.

"BOYS!" said Barkin.

The boys braked, ditched their bikes, and ran up to the man.

"Principal Barkin!" said Niles.

"Now, now," said Barkin. "I'm not your principal any longer. Call me Barry."

"Barry," said Miles, "we need—"

"Miles Murphy, the invitation to call me Barry was extended to Niles. You may call me Mr. Barkin."

"Mr. Barkin," said Miles, "we need—"

Barkin frowned. "That didn't sound right either. Miles, why don't you go ahead and call me Former Principal Barkin."

"Former Principal Barkin," said Miles, "we need—"

"Niles!" said Barkin. "Where's your sash?"

"Josh is the School Helper now," said Niles.

"Josh Barkin?"

"Yes."

"Well, that doesn't make much sense."

"Things are a lot different now."

"That boy never tells me anything," said Barkin.

"Former Principal Barkin," said Miles, "we need to talk to you."

Barkin checked a digital watch. "Can it wait until after

I've completed my first flight? Civil twilight's in twenty-five minutes."

Up close, the hang glider appeared dangerously shabby. Niles wasn't sure what a glider was supposed to look like, but he was pretty sure it wasn't this:

"I'm worried that's not safe," Miles said.

"*The Spirit of Yawnee Valley Science and Letters Academy?* I built her myself! She soars! Or she will soar, I'm fairly sure.

She'll soar around on the wind and take me into that wild blue yonder."

He pointed to the blackness below.

"That wild black yonder." Barkin pulled on his mustache. "I was really hoping to take off before now, while the yonder was still blue, but I had to make some last-minute adjustments. The poles on the wings kept coming loose."

"That's what I mean, Former Principal Barkin. I'm not sure that's good."

Barkin scoffed. "Miles Murphy, did you become a hang glider expert since I left school? Did Ms. Shandy add a hang gliding element to her unit on the Mayans?"

"No."

"Of course she didn't! Because Ms. Shandy is a fine social studies teacher, and hang gliding is completely irrelevant to Mayan history! How is Ms. Shandy, by the way?"

"She's good," said Miles.

"Good. That's good. Now, if you'll excuse me, Miles Murphy, I will prepare for takeoff, confident, because I have been studying hang glider making for the past two weeks and you have not."

"I don't think it's good that the poles came loose either," said Niles.

"No?" Barkin's face became plaintive. "No, I suppose it's not."

He sat down gingerly. Another pole came loose and the wing tore.

He removed a notebook from his fanny pack and crossed something out. "Looks like I'm lousy at hang gliders too."

"What's that?" Niles asked.

"It's my project list. I've been trying my hand at hobbies since I left school, but I'm terrible at everything. Terrible at soapmaking, terrible at jigsaw puzzles, terrible at stand-up comedy. Terrible at close-up magic and sewing and lapidary."

"Lapidary?"

"The art of cutting gemstones. I'm terrible at it. The only thing I ever enjoyed was being a principal, and I was terrible at that too."

"You were a great principal!" said Miles.

"Thank you, Miles. That means a lot, even coming from you. But I *was* terrible. I couldn't even suss out the scoundrel who was committing all those pranks at our school."

"That's actually why we're here." Niles took a big breath. "Barry, it was us."

SO LET ME GET THIS STRAIGHT." Barry Barkin was still strapped into his glider, pacing anxiously and awkwardly in the underbrush. "You come and tell me that you are both pranksters, which is no surprise when it comes to you, Miles Murphy, but is a considerable surprise in regards to you, Niles Sparks, and while I am still reeling from the news, you invite me to join this secret society you've set up, the Terrible Twos?"

"The Terrible Two," said Niles.

"The Terrible Twos is what you call toddlers," said Miles.

"Right. The Terrible Two," said Barkin. "It's a little confusing."

"It's not really confusing," said Miles.

"Well, it is," said Barkin. "If I'm going to join this little group, and I seriously doubt that I am, we're going to have to do something about that name. May I suggest"—Barkin paused for effect—"the Terrible Threes!"

"You mean the Terrible Three," said Niles.

"Right. Yes. The Terrible Three!"

"We're not changing our name," said Miles.

"But there'd be three of us!"

"It would just be for one prank," said Miles. "We need you to help us get your dad."

"That's my other problem with this group," said Barkin. "Does it have to be a pranking society? Wouldn't it be better if it were, say, a community service organization?"

"No," said Miles.

"I sort of think of pranking as a community service," said Niles.

"HA!" Barkin didn't say "HA!" as much as the "HA!" exploded out from deep inside him. He then collected himself and tapped his mustache. "That's very interesting."

Barkin tramped around some more in the scrub.

"Boys, I just don't know. Maybe Yawnee Valley Science and Letters Academy is better off without me. Let's face it— my father is a far better principal than I ever was."

Niles shook his head. "Your dad is an awful principal. He's taken the joy out of school."

Barkin looked sorrowful. "But school should be a place of joy!"

"Exactly," said Miles. "And it was when you were principal."

Barkin beamed. "In what ways did I make school joyful, Miles Murphy?"

"Well," said Miles. "Um. You always turned purple when we pulled pranks."

Niles shot Miles a stunned glance.

"Excuse me?" said Barkin.

"Yeah!" said Niles. "Whenever something would go wrong, you always got angry and turned purple."

Barkin was starting to go a little purple right now.

"Because you cared so much," Miles said.

"Ah!" said Barkin. "I see what you mean now, Miles, even though you phrased it in a characteristically clunky manner. I did care. I do care."

"Your dad doesn't care at all," said Niles. "He only cares about power."

"Yes, that's true," said Barkin. "And I only mostly care about power."

"We have to get you your job back," said Niles. "It's our fault you lost it. We're sorry."

"Really sorry," said Miles.

Barkin gave Miles and Niles a truly warm smile. "It's not your fault, boys. It's my father's. But prank him? A pranking principal . . ."

"Former principal," said Miles.

"Think of it as a project!" said Niles.

"But I'm terrible at all my projects," said Barkin.

"Well," said Miles, "what if you're great at being Terrible?"

"The Terrible Twos," Barkin mused.

"Two," said Miles.

"The Terrible Two," Barkin mused.

He considered the proposition.

"All right, I'm in."

Niles smiled. "Raise your left hand."

Once Barkin was sworn in, the Terrible Two (known to some, at least temporarily, as the Terrible Three) got down to business.

"Does your dad have any weaknesses?" Miles asked.

"None!" said Barkin proudly.

"Please," said Niles. "There must be something."

"Nope!" said Barkin. "He is the very model of principal power!"

"You're thinking like a principal," said Miles. "You need to think like a prankster."

Barkin wrinkled his nose and screwed his eyes shut.

"This is very difficult!" he said.

"Think!" said Niles.

"ARRGHGHGHGHHHHHHHHHHHHHHHH!"
Barkin's cry echoed through the quarry. He opened his eyes and gave the boys a sheepish look. "There is . . . something," he said.

"Yeah?" said Miles.

"It's explosive," said Barkin.

"That's good," said Niles.

"It's a secret," said Barkin. "A family secret. Except my father never told it to me, and I am his family. It's something I only learned once I became principal and gained access to my father's permanent record."

Miles and Niles leaned forward.

"My father," said Barkin, "does not have a perfect attendance record."

Miles rolled his eyes. "I don't think that—"

Barkin continued, his voice hushed. "His record was almost perfect. But as my father always says, there is no such thing as 'almost perfect.' On his very last day at Yawnee Valley Science and Letters Academy, he was . . . he was . . . I don't think I should say."

"What?" said Niles.

"He was pantsed. By another student. A ruffian named Nick Vella, who for many years ran the sporting goods store in town. In retrospect, it's clear now why we drove all the way to Lakeville for sneakers, which of course was far out of our way and—"

"Wait," said Niles. "You're saying somebody *pantsed* your dad."

"I'm afraid so," said Barkin. "Apparently he was so mortified he went home early. And he skipped the graduation ceremony. The school had to mail him his diploma."

"That's why the belt and suspenders!" said Miles.

"I think we can work with this," said Niles. "Principal Barkin, how often do you go over to your parents' house?"

Principal Barkin's eyes widened.

"Oh, this is terrible," he said. "Oh, this is wonderful."

THERE WERE NO CLUMPS when the students filed into the auditorium on the last day of school, just an orderly line, single file. Josh Barkin stood just inside the entrance, inspecting the students and making indecipherable notes on his clipboard. Everything appeared to be in perfect order, but when Ms. Shandy's homeroom took their seats, two students were missing. Miles and Niles were hidden in the wings of the stage, crouching behind some props from last year's production of *Peter Pan*.

The assembly was scheduled to start at 2:00 P.M. At 1:59, Gus wheeled out the prank sign and set a pitcher of water on the podium. A minute later Bertrand Barkin, clad as always in a dark suit, pants belted and braced, took the stage.

"Children," he said. "Congratulations. Congratulations to you and congratulations to me. Today is my 120th school day as principal, and things have gone exactly as I expected. The pranking epidemic has been quashed. I am proud to say we have gone 119 and five-sixths days without a practical joke."

There was tepid applause.

"Thank you. Thank you. Back in November, I stood on this stage and promised you a bit of fun. And that is a promise I intend to keep. So get ready to give a warm welcome to a special visitor from the district office. It's time to spend our last hour of school with Sammy the Safety Lobster!"

The applause was even more tepid.

A man in a purple lobster suit entered from stage right. As he passed Miles and Niles, he gave them a little salute with one of his claws.

"This clever crustacean," said Bertrand Barkin, reading from a piece of paper, "is here to give you some hot tips on how to stay cool—and safe—all summer long. Hi, Sammy!"

The lobster gave an exaggerated wave and clicked his pincers.

"Here we go," Niles said.

The Terrible Two removed a bag of fireworks from each of their backpacks.

Sammy the Safety Lobster waddled dizzily toward the podium, where Bertrand Barkin stood frozen and grinning.

"One," said Miles.

The lobster sidled up to Bertrand Barkin. Mr. Sykes came up onstage with an old cell phone to get a picture for the district newsletter.

"Two," said Niles.

The lobster put his arm around the principal, resting his left claw on Bertrand's waist, right where his belt and suspenders met.

"Three," said Miles.

Sammy removed his purple lobster head, revealing the purple human head of Barry Barkin. His hair and mustache were damp with sweat.

There were many gasps.

Barry Barkin edged his father away from the podium and shouted into the microphone.

"STUDENTS! FACULTY! STAFF! IT IS I, BARRY BARKIN, YOUR FORMER PRINCIPAL."

Bertrand Barkin puckered his lips in disgust. "Never

in all my life," he said, "did I think a Barkin would sink so low as to become a safety lobster."

"I APOLOGIZE FOR INTERRUPTING THIS IMPORTANT ASSEMBLY, BUT I AM HERE TO FOIL A PRANK THAT WAS MERE SECONDS FROM BEING COMMITTED."

"NONSENSE," hissed Bertrand Barkin. "Students do not prank now that I am principal."

"THEN WHAT DO YOU CALL THIS?" said Barry Barkin. "BOYS. COME ON OUT. THE GIG IS UP. OR THE JIG IS UP. WHICH IS IT? THE GIG OR THE JIG. THE PRANK IS OVER."

Miles and Niles, shoulders hunched, slunk onto the stage.

Miles glared at Barry Barkin.

Niles shook his head.

"WHILE I HAVE BEEN ON AN INVOLUNTARY, INDEFINITE LEAVE OF ABSENCE," said Principal Barkin, "I HAVE CONTINUED TO INVESTIGATE THE PRANK EPIDEMIC. AND I AM PROUD TO SAY THAT I HAVE UNCOVERED A SECRET PRANKING SOCIETY. THESE TWO RUFFIANS COMPOSE A PRANKING DUO KNOWN AS THE TERRIBLE TWOS."

"Two," said Miles.

"THE TERRIBLE TWO," said Barry Barkin. "BOYS, DUMP OUT THOSE BAGS."

"But, sir," Niles pleaded.

"DO IT."

"Come on," said Miles.

"NOW, MILES MURPHY."

Fireworks spilled forth onto the stage.

"Well, well," said Holly, sitting in the audience. "Look at those samizdatchiks."

"FIREWORKS. AT A SAFETY ASSEMBLY. IT'S DIABOLICAL."

Meanwhile, at his place two paces from the podium, Bertrand Barkin's face had taken on a fuchsia tint of its own.

"THERE ARE SOME WHO DOUBTED MY ABILITY TO SNIFF OUT PRANKS," Barkin continued. "TO THEM, I SAY, 'I HAVE A PRINCIPAL'S NOSE!' AND I ALSO SAY, 'CAN I PLEASE HAVE MY JOB BACK?'"

Bertrand Barkin could feel he was losing the room. A reptilian cool came into his eyes. Softly, he cleared his throat.

Barry Barkin turned and looked at his dad.

Bertrand Barkin reached over and poured himself a glass of water.

Panic flooded Barry Barkin's face. "Father! No!" he screamed, knocking the glass out of Bertrand's hand with his giant claw. Water spilled all over the principal's black suit.

There was a low rumbling in the crowd.

"You fool," said Bertrand. "You clumsy fool. Why did you do that?"

"Father," said Barry, "these kids have been known to spike beverages with capsicum from blazing hot peppers!"

"Don't you think I know that?" Bertrand looked down. One great thing about dark trousers was that they hid spills well, but he could use this accident to his advantage. "Step aside," he said.

Barry abandoned the podium.

Bertrand smiled. His son had given up the power position. He looked at the stage—a sweaty man in a headless lobster suit and a pair of exposed pranksters. This circus needed to come to an end. Now.

"Children, let's take a moment to silently express our gratitude for your former principal. In fact"—he leaned forward now—"let's take a two-minute moment of complete silence to honor him for the good work he did when he was the head of this school."

Ninety seconds was all it took to suck the excitement back out of the room.

"If only my son had done his job when he had it, he might never have lost it," Bertrand Barkin said. "Still, we can be glad he stopped this practical joke in its tracks. The assembly, obviously, is canceled. You will return to your classrooms and clean out your desks. Then you will clean the tops of your desks, and then you will clean the bottoms. But first, this prank foiled, it gives me great pleasure to turn over the final number on our prank sign."

Bertrand Barkin sneered at the two boys onstage, then stepped out from behind the podium and crossed over to the sign.

The assembly was awestruck.

Every girl and boy, man and woman in the crowd could not believe what they were seeing.

"Principal Barkin's PANTS fell APART!" said Stuart. "And FELL DOWN!"

Miles and Niles smiled, but Barry Barkin was the first to laugh.

Barry Barkin's laugh was loud and warm and deep, and it

was joined by snickers, snorts, and guffaws from the students of Yawnee Valley Science and Letters Academy, and most of the teachers too (including Ms. Shandy, who may have laughed the loudest).

Bertrand Barkin turned a wild eye on his son, and then on Miles, and finally on Niles. He couldn't figure out what had happened, or what was happening, or what to do next. For the first time he could remember, things were out of control. His face was the color of a field violet.

"So much for Principal Invincible," said Holly, loud enough for him to hear.

Bertrand Barkin waved a wild finger at the auditorium. "I'LL BE REVENGED ON THE WHOLE PACK OF YOU!" he shouted. Then he ran off the stage, the pieces of his pants trailing on the ground behind him.

Watching his father go, Barry Barkin said quietly, so only Miles and Niles could hear, "You are dismissed."

Chapter
25

BARRY BARKIN, formerly Former Principal Barkin, was now Acting Principal Barkin. Tomorrow, at an emergency meeting of the school board, he'd be fully reinstated. For now, he was happily engaged in one of his favorite principal duties: overseeing after-school detention.

It was 3:30 P.M. and the last day of school had just ended, and today there were only two students in detention. (You know who they are.)

Miles and Niles sat side by side, surrounded by empty desks. Acting Principal Barkin was at the head of the class with his feet up.

He tossed a spool of Wash-a-Way thread to Niles, who caught it.

"Amazing stuff," said Acting Principal Barkin.

"You weren't terrible at sewing," said Niles. "Sewing and pranking—that's two projects I'd call successful."

Acting Principal Barkin pulled out a notebook from his Acting Principal Pack and made some notes. "That's a good point, Niles. A very good point."

Miles checked his watch. "Principal Barkin, we don't actually have to stay for detention, do we?"

"Of course you do," said Barkin. "You're pranksters. Consider yourself lucky it's the last day of school. Your punishment is: detention every day until the last day of school. Luckily, as I've already said, that day is today."

"Come on," said Miles. "It's summer vacation. We got you your job back. Cut us some slack."

"Slack," said Barkin, "is something I never cut." His grin was downright mischievous. "I do, however, sometimes cut slacks. Get it? Because last week I *cut* my father's *slacks* and then sewed them up with that thread—"

"No, yeah, we get it," said Miles.

"Good prank, good prank," said Acting Principal Barkin.

Minutes passed. Miles sighed. "What are we supposed to do now?"

"Read a book. Twiddle your thumbs. Start your memoirs."

Niles pulled a copy of the *Collected Poems of Emily Dickinson* from his backpack.

"I didn't bring a book," said Miles.

Niles took out a copy of *Matilda* and gave it to his friend.

Barkin stood up. "Oh! I almost forgot. Before you settle in."

Barkin crossed the room and opened the door. "Gus!" he shouted.

Gus, slyly smiling, wheeled in the prank sign. It still read 119.

"We almost made it to 120," Barkin said. "But I'm afraid this sign needs to be reset."

Miles nodded at Niles. "You do it."

Niles walked up to the front of the classroom.

His hand trembled as he flipped the digits.

"Thank you, Gus," said Barkin. "Put this away somewhere. The basement."

Gus nodded.

Watching the sign go, Niles thought he might cry.

"Now!" said Principal Barkin, looking around the room. "Can we do that secret handshake? The one I saw you do at the meeting? What was it? This?"

He held up two fingers. "Oh!" he said, looking at his hand. "I get it."

Miles got up and joined the pair at the front of the classroom.

"Just this once," said Barkin, "could we do it like this?"

He held up a third finger.

Miles and Niles looked at each other.

"Sure," Miles said.

ABOUT *the* AUTHORS

MAC BARNETT is a *New York Times* bestselling author of many books for children, including *Extra Yarn*, illustrated by Jon Klassen, which won a 2013 Caldecott Honor and the 2012 *Boston Globe–Horn Book* Award for Excellence in Picture Books; *Sam & Dave Dig a Hole*, also illustrated by Jon Klassen and a 2015 Caldecott Honor winner; and *Battle Bunny*, written with Jon Scieszka and illustrated by Matthew Myers. He also writes the Brixton Brothers series of mystery novels.

JORY JOHN is the author of the picture books *Goodnight Already!* (with Benji Davies) and *I Will Chomp You* (with Bob Shea) and coauthor of the national bestseller *All My Friends Are Dead*; a sequel, *All My Friends Are STILL Dead*; and *Pirate's Log: A Handbook for Aspiring Swashbucklers*, among other books. Jory spent six years as programs director at 826 Valencia, a nonprofit educational center in San Francisco.

KEVIN CORNELL is the illustrator of several children's books, including *Count the Monkeys* and *Mustache!* by Mac Barnett, and the Chicken Squad series by Doreen Cronin. Most recently, he wrote and illustrated the picture book *Go to Sleep, Monster!* He resides in Philadelphia, where he, his wife, and a brand-new Persian rug are pranked several times a day by their dog.

FOR DAVE EGGERS
—MB AND JJ

Library of Congress Cataloging-in-Publication Data

Barnett, Mac, author.

The terrible two get worse / Mac Barnett, Jory John ; illustrated by Kevin Cornell.

pages cm

Sequel to: The terrible two.

Summary: "Friends and pranking partners Miles and Niles face a tough challenge when their favorite goat and nemesis, Principal Barkin, is replaced by his stern, no-nonsense father, Former Principal Barkin, who turns the school into boot camp." —Provided by publisher.

ISBN 978-1-4197-1680-5 (hardback) — ISBN 978-1-61312-839-8 (ebook)

[1. Practical jokes—Fiction. 2. Tricks—Fiction. 3. School principals—Fiction. 4. Schools—Fiction. 5. Friendship—Fiction. 6. Humorous stories.] I. John, Jory, author. II. Cornell, Kevin, illustrator. III. Title.

PZ7.B26615Tg 2016

[Fic]—dc23

2015011114

Amulet Books are available at special discounts when purchased in quantity for premiums and promotions as well as fundraising or educational use. Special editions can also be created to specification. For details, contact specialsales@abramsbooks.com or the address below.

ABRAMS

THE ART OF BOOKS SINCE 1949

115 West 18th Street

New York, NY 10011

www.abramsbooks.com